Frosted Window Panes

A Modern *Pride and Prejudice* Christmas Novella

by
KARA LOUISE

ISBN-13: 979-8849005522
ISBN-10: 8849005522

Cover images by Dreamstime.com
Cover design by Kara Louise

Printed in the United States of America

Library of Congress Cataloguing-in-Publication Data

Kara Louise
Frosted Window Panes

Published by Heartworks Publication

A Note to My Readers

I always like to express my great appreciation for all who contribute to my books. I am greatly indebted to Jane Austen, of course, who gave us her wonderful stories and the characters that many of us have come to adore. Her gifted writing is what inspires me.

I would also like to thank the three ladies who gave this book several read-throughs and provided invaluable input. They are Mary Anne Hinz, Anastasia Bierman, and Jayme Novara. I really appreciate all their help in improving this book. I also want to thank my sister, Donna Natale, who was the first one to give eyes to this story and also did the final look through.
Her suggestions helped me immensely.

Finally, I am greatly appreciative of you, my readers, who chose to read this book. There are several things in this book that are near and dear to my heart, and I hope that you were drawn into this story as much as I was drawn to write it.

I hope you will enjoy this modern *Pride and Prejudice* inspired Christmas novella.

Kara Louise

Chapter 1

November

"Why did I ever agree to do this?" Elizabeth Bennet asked herself softly as she glanced down at her watch.

"Is something wrong, Miss Bennet?" Kamie Etzler asked.

Elizabeth looked up at Kamie, one of the teachers at her tutoring center, and gave her head a quick shake.

"No, nothing is wrong. I am trying to decide whether it was wise to suggest doing something with my sister this evening." She felt like rolling her eyes, but she refrained. In truth, she had insisted upon doing it, while Jane most likely preferred that she had not.

"I'm sure you made the right decision," said Laura Porter, another teacher.

In addition to her concern over this evening's plans, there was the phone call from Mr. Forster. She had not told Kamie or Laura about the disappointing news he had given her and hoped she would be able to figure something out.

"Laura and I are almost finished washing and drying the dishes. Is there anything else you'd like us to do before we leave?" Kamie asked.

"No. There isn't much left that needs to be done. You can leave when you're finished."

"Are you sure? We can stay if you want."

"When will my mommy get here?"

Elizabeth walked over to little Vanessa Morell and gently placed her hands on the six-year-old's shoulders. The young girl had become increasingly distraught since the last child had been picked up fifteen minutes earlier.

"I hope she wasn't in an accident." Her voice trembled.

Elizabeth gently squeezed Vanessa's shoulders. "I am sure she is just stuck in traffic and will be here shortly. There is no need to worry."

When Laura and Kamie finished cleaning up, they retrieved their belongings and said goodbye to Elizabeth and Vanessa.

Elizabeth closed and locked the door behind them and looked down at her watch again. She hoped Vanessa was not sensing the anxiety she was feeling about her plans for the evening. She hoped to have left by now to allow her plenty of time to get ready, but it appeared that wouldn't happen tonight.

Mrs. Morell finally arrived and apologized for being late. She hadn't been able to get out of a meeting, and her phone's battery had died, otherwise she would have called.

Elizabeth assured Mrs. Morell she understood, and when the woman and her daughter walked out, Elizabeth let out a long breath as she looked around at the things that still needed to be done before she left for home.

Any other day, she would have stayed to hang some still wet paintings to the wall, taken the trash out, and finished some paperwork before leaving for the apartment she shared with Jane. She decided to leave the paintings on the table where they would be dry by morning. The paperwork could wait another day. She picked up a few papers and threw them into the trash can as she went to her office to retrieve her purse and coat.

She walked to the front door and then turned around to look back at the room. Satisfied with how things looked, she opened the door and stepped out, locking it behind her and giving it a good tug to make sure it was secure.

The fresh scent of a recent rain filled the air as she briskly walked to her car. It was November, and the days were short, but at least it was not cold enough to snow. There would be enough of that in the coming months.

Elizabeth started her car and let it warm up while she called her sister to let her know she was running late but should be there within thirty minutes.

"All right," Jane replied. "Don't drive too fast. The streets might still be a little wet from the rain we had earlier."

"I'll be careful. I'll see you when I get home."

Elizabeth ended the call, proud of herself that she had refrained from asking Jane whether she had changed her mind about going out with a man she only met yesterday in line at a deli.

Jane was always concerned about Elizabeth's safety working in Meryton Heights, as well as the drive to and from. Elizabeth, on the other hand, tended to worry about Jane, who was so trusting of everyone. Elizabeth was not particularly pleased that her sister had agreed to go out with this man without knowing anything about him.

"I think he is the one!" Jane had said yesterday when she told Elizabeth about how she met Charles.

"How could you even know that after one brief encounter?" Elizabeth had asked her.

Elizabeth came to a red light and tapped her fingers on the steering wheel to the beat of the song playing on the radio. The couple planned to meet at a restaurant, and she was grateful Jane had agreed to let her join them. She could check out Charles Bingley herself. "Well, at least he was still willing to meet Jane for dinner after she told him she was bringing me along." She let out a laugh. "He does have that in his favor."

They would be going to Derby Steakhouse, so if the company wasn't desirable, at least the food would be delicious!

Elizabeth pulled into her parking space at their apartment and hurried up to the second floor. Her key was in her hand, but she had no need to use it. Jane opened the door for her.

"Hi!" Jane's face was rosy and glowing, her eyes were bright, and her smile was bigger than Elizabeth remembered seeing in a long time.

"Hi, Jane," Elizabeth replied with a chuckle. "You weren't by any chance watching for me, were you?"

Jane tilted her head. "What makes you ask that?"

Elizabeth held up the key in her hand. "Oh, perhaps it was how quickly you opened the door even before I could use my key." She stepped in. "You are really looking forward to this evening, aren't you?"

Jane clasped her hands tightly. "Oh, I've been waiting all day! I couldn't keep my mind focused on my work! I can't wait for you to meet Charles."

Elizabeth took off her coat and put it, along with her purse, on a chair. "I would surmise you have been waiting all day to see Charles, not for me to meet him."

"Both!" Jane assured her.

"Well, if you don't mind, I need to get ready. I don't want to meet Charles in a blouse covered in paint." She pointed to a few smudges.

"We still have time, but I am certain Charles wouldn't mind."

As Elizabeth walked to her bedroom, Jane's phone rang. Elizabeth turned and watched as Jane glanced at the phone. A smile lit her face.

"Hello, Charles."

Elizabeth leaned against the wall and watched as Jane listened in silence, nodding occasionally.

Jane finally spoke. "Me, too. Oh. You would rather go to Hobbs on the Hill?" She stole a glance at her sister.

Elizabeth shook her head and began waving her arms. She hurried over to her. "Not Hobbs on the Hill!" she whispered vehemently.

"Um, that would be nice, but... if you don't mind, I think I would prefer Derby's." She sent her sister a reassuring smile. "OK." After a pause, she said, "A friend?"

Elizabeth's eyes widened and then narrowed.

"Sure, we'll see you soon." Jane turned the phone off and lifted her eyes. "Don't worry. We're still going to Derby's. But why are you so opposed to Hobbs on the Hill? I hear it's nice."

Elizabeth grasped her sister's hands, giving them a squeeze. "My dearest sister, he wants to impress you by taking you to an exclusive restaurant that doesn't even list its prices on the menu. I wouldn't be surprised if you have to pay for the water! Hobbs on the Hill! Hah! You know why everyone calls it *Snobs* on the Hill?"

"Lizzy, I'm sure not everyone calls it that. It supposedly has delicious food, wonderful atmosphere, the most amazing view of the city, and apparently the hotel up there is the finest around!"

Elizabeth released her hands. "I'm sure it is a wonderful restaurant, has an amazing view, and a fine hotel which we have no need for, but Charles needs to impress you with himself, not a restaurant or its food or the atmosphere."

Jane let out a sigh. "I know you'll like him, Lizzy. Just wait." She turned to sit down, but Elizabeth took her by the arm, bringing her to a halt.

"What was this about a friend?"

Jane's face paled, and she winced. "He... he said he is also bringing someone – a friend."

"Oh, Jane. You know there is nothing I dislike more than being set up on a blind date."

"Lizzy, this isn't a blind date. It's not any kind of date!" She gave a shrug. "But you know, if you don't want to go, you don't have to."

Elizabeth wagged her finger. "Jane, you barely met this guy. I am sure he is a fine gentleman, but you are so trusting while I tend to be a bit more cautious." She leaned in and laughed. "Just humor me. You won't even notice that I am there!"

~~*

It began to drizzle as Elizabeth drove the two of them to the restaurant. They pulled into the small parking lot behind the steakhouse, but there were no parking places available. When the dark gray clouds suddenly released a deluge of water, Elizabeth reached for her umbrella, but couldn't find it.

"Oh, dear! I must have left my umbrella at work. Since I'll have to park on the street, I'll drop you off in front, so you don't have to walk to the restaurant in the rain." She looked both ways before pulling back out and then turned to smile at Jane. "That way you won't be all washed out for your Charles."

"Oh, but Lizzy..."

Elizabeth put up her hand. "I won't hear another word from you. You're the one who is meeting someone and hoping to make a good impression." She pulled to a stop in front. "I'll be back shortly."

Jane scrambled out of the car, and Elizabeth pulled ahead, keeping her eyes open for a close parking spot. She turned the windshield wipers on to their highest speed as the rain fell harder.

She found a parking space over a block away. She reached around again for her umbrella just in case it was not in the normal pocket on the side of her door.

"Looks like it's just me and the rain!"

Elizabeth sat for a few moments before she stepped out. She let out a long breath and looked out the window at the rain pouring down. She was tempted to just go home. She really should have trusted Jane's judgment. "Oh, well, I'm here. I might as well at least go in and meet this guy!" She opened the door, pulled her coat over her head, and looked down as she hurried towards the restaurant, hoping she wouldn't collide into someone.

Unfortunately, she did, just as she reached the restaurant.

"Sorry," she said, slipping under the canopy at the front door.

"They really ought to have valet parking," was the gruff response from the gentleman, who stepped underneath it, as well.

She looked up to see a tall, well-dressed man, who had not forgotten an umbrella. He shook it out and closed it. By his attire, Elizabeth thought he should be going to a fancy restaurant instead of this one.

"Well, it's not *Snobs* on the Hill," she said with a soft chuckle. She winced. *Did I say that out loud?*

"Pardon me?" the gentleman asked, with a look of annoyance.

Elizabeth gave her head a shake. He didn't seem to appreciate her comment, and she cleared her throat. "It's not… never mind. A little rain – or walk – won't hurt anyone." The rain was the least of her worries right now.

The gentleman grumbled and walked up to the door, opening it for her. As she walked past him, she caught a scent of his cologne. The cologne may have been heavenly, but he certainly was not.

She stepped inside and looked about, hoping her eyes would quickly adjust to the dimly lit room. She could sense the gentleman behind her, and imagined he was doing the same. She soon saw Jane sitting next to a nice-looking man. They were in the waiting area by themselves, and she had a ray of hope that he had decided not to bring his friend. Jane turned, and upon noticing her, gave the gentleman, whom Elizabeth assumed was Charles, a nudge. A wide smile lit his face, he said something to Jane, and the two stood.

Elizabeth walked over, still sensing - and smelling - the gentleman behind her. When she came up to them, Jane reached out and took her hand. Charles extended his hand, but Elizabeth thought it odd he was not extending it to her. When a hand from behind her took his, she cringed. Of all the people Charles had invited, it had to be Mr. No-Valet-Parking!

Introductions were made, and the gentleman who had walked in with her was Will Darcy. As the foursome waited to be called, they shared a little about themselves and their occupations.

"I'm an accountant for a large web design company and have been with them for four years," Charles began. "It's a great place to work, and I love what I do." He turned to Jane. "And I don't know how Jane and I could have worked so near each other all this time and never met before yesterday!" He reached over and took Jane's hand. "You go next, Jane."

"All right. For three years I have worked as an executive assistant to a group of lawyers in a law firm specializing in litigation and contract breaches." She shared a little bit more about her responsibilities.

"Do you ever plan to become a lawyer yourself?" Will asked.

She gave a shrug. "I am not sure. I enjoy what I do and that I don't have to take my work home with me as so many of the lawyers have to do."

Charles let out a laugh. "That sounds like Will! He's always working!"

Elizabeth had noticed that his friend had frequently looked at his watch or down at his phone as the others talked. She wondered if he had some other place he needed – or wanted – to be!

"Tell them what you do, Will."

"I'0ve been with my family's company, Darcy Enterprises, since my late teens. It was a company that my late grandfather founded over forty years ago."

He paused and didn't seem inclined to continue, but Charles jumped in. "He is being modest. He is CEO of Darcy Enterprises and has been in that position for about four years now."

"That is very impressive!" Jane said, casting a quick glance at Elizabeth, lifting her brows.

Before Elizabeth had the opportunity to talk about her job, their party was called, and they followed the waitress to a round table at the back of the restaurant. Elizabeth walked ahead of Will, and she could almost feel his contempt for this place. At one point she thought she heard him let out a huff.

Derby Steakhouse was not fancy, and they hadn't updated their decor in at least twenty years. The only thing that could be considered fancy was the string of white twinkling lights draped around a small, polished wood dancing floor. Unfortunately, there was no band, just a jukebox where patrons could select the music they wanted to dance to. They did have delicious, but reasonably priced steaks and excellent service.

The waitress set the menus down on their small round table. Elizabeth took the chair on one side of Jane, and Charles on the other. Will sat between his friend and Elizabeth.

She was determined to decide for herself just how perfect Charles Bingley was for Jane. As for his friend, she already had her mind made up about him.

Chapter 2

As they opened their menus, Will asked, "Is anything good here?"

Elizabeth grimaced. "As a matter of fact, the steaks are delicious and always cooked to perfection." She sent him a forced smile. "They will cook them any way you like." She lifted a brow. "I would surmise that you prefer your steaks cooked rare – or very well done."

Will leaned back in his chair and crossed his arms. "Medium rare, actually."

When the waitress came back to take their order, Elizabeth ordered her steak medium rare, as well.

Elizabeth's phone rang, and she pulled it out to look at it. Seeing who it was, she turned it off and set it down.

The waitress took their order, and Elizabeth listened as Jane and Charles talked. She noticed how different the two men were from each other and couldn't help wondering how they could be such close friends.

Charles had a smile that never faded and eyes that sparkled, seeking eye contact with the person who was speaking. As he spoke, he looked from one person to another, even if his conversation was directed at only one person, which was usually Jane. It was as if he was including everyone in the conversation. He was lively and engaging, but he was not at all overbearing. He was dressed nicely, but more casually than his friend. His hair was cut short, but he had a few unruly curls that stood up on end. His hands looked like he often worked with them.

Elizabeth took a quick look at the man sitting next to her. He was handsome, to be sure, with his designer suit, manicured nails and styled hair, and a dimple that took Elizabeth by surprise the first time she noticed it. It was not one of those dimples that marks the face all the time but showed itself only on occasion. His teeth were white - she couldn't help but wonder if they were real. But it was his eyes. They seemed to have a depth to them - not only in the intensity of his gaze, but in an understanding of the world around him. When he looked at you, it was almost as if he was seeking to understand who you really were; trying to determine whether you were wearing a mask. She wondered if he was wearing a mask that hid who he was.

As Elizabeth watched her sister and Charles talk, she couldn't help but smile at Jane's serene countenance, her subdued delight as they conversed and discovered their mutual interests, and her sister's occasional glance at her, as if rubbing it in that he was everything she believed him to be. She had to admit that based on her first impression of him, he did seem to be exactly as Jane described. His friend, however… She stole a quick glance at him. She was grateful she and Will were not on a date.

As if knowing she was thinking about him, Will unexpectedly turned and met her gaze. "We never heard what it is you do, Elizabeth."

His apparent interest startled her. "I… I run an after-school tutoring center northeast of downtown… in Meryton Heights."

"Meryton Heights? I see."

Oh, I'm sure you see, she thought.

She saw his eyes twitch. Could he be inwardly censuring her for doing something he would consider beneath him? Working with people who had very little, who worried where their next meal might come from, and who had to do their shopping in the second-hand store? It was likely he didn't give a second thought to spending his money wherever and whenever he wanted.

"What is the name?"

It took her a moment to realize he had asked a question.

"Your daycare…"

"Oh! No, it isn't a daycare." She drew in a breath to calm herself. The one thing she hated was for people to refer to it as a daycare, when they did so much more academically than just babysit children. "It's called the Providence Readiness Excel Program Academy."

"We call it PREP Academy or PREP for short," added Jane.

"All who come are required to do schoolwork, and we help when needed." All eyes were on her, and she had a sudden urge to make a good impression. "I find it rewarding to see the progress made by some of our boys and girls who have been a part of this program since kindergarten. Many of them need special attention, and the schools don't have the manpower, resources, or time to give them."

Jane leaned in. "She is absolutely wonderful working with them."

Will tilted his head, and his eyes were fixed on her as she spoke. His brows narrowed slightly.

She was perturbed that he likely thought it was not an esteemed occupation for a lady. "It isn't just babysitting if that's what you're thinking. We pride ourselves on giving our students what they need to succeed. Many have learning disabilities, and they don't always get the direction they need in the public schools. Right now, we only take children through elementary school, but I hope to expand and open it up to middle and high schoolers."

The smile on Charles's face expressed his enthusiasm. "I think that is awesome!"

Elizabeth returned his smile. "I have big plans for it. I hope someday – with the right amount of space and staff – to offer sports, music, dance, and art, in addition to what we do now, which is tutoring basic school subjects. I want to be able to give them the opportunity to participate in things that interest them. I want to open doors to them that will expose them to something new – something they perhaps hadn't considered or did not have the means to take part in."

"Don't forget the computer lab," Jane said as she turned to Charles. "That's something she would like to implement soon."

"What do you charge the families for these opportunities?" Will leaned back again, crossing his arms.

Elizabeth stifled a grimace at his question. She knew how the wealthy are always thinking of money – and the making of it. He was likely no different, and his posture confirmed it.

"I charge on a sliding scale depending on the income of the family, as well as some other factors. Someday, I would like to be able to offer scholarships to those who need it."

Will leaned forward, lifting a brow. "You have lofty dreams."

"And success often comes from such dreams." She felt herself stiffen. "It isn't everyone who can be born into a successful family or career." She grabbed her purse. "If you will excuse me, I need to go to the ladies room."

"I'll come with you," Jane said.

As they stepped around the partition behind their table that took them to the restroom, Elizabeth remembered she had left her phone on the table.

"Oh, I forgot my phone. I'm going to go back and get it. George called earlier and I want to text him back while we're in there."

When she stepped back around the short partition wall, the two men were talking.

"So, my good friend, what do you think?" Charles asked.

Elizabeth paused.

"I confess I'm surprised you brought her here. Why didn't you take her to Hobbs on the Hill, as I recommended? This isn't the best restaurant to impress a lady on a first date."

"I suggested it, but Jane said she preferred to come here. She says it is very good." Charles looked around him. "Not the best atmosphere, I admit, but I wasn't asking about the restaurant, what do you think of Jane?"

Elizabeth watched Will take in a deep breath. "Jane is pretty. I grant you that."

"She is an angel!" Charles declared.

Will shook his head. "There is more to a lady's suitability than her appearance."

"She is the sweetest girl I have ever met!" Charles took a sip of his drink. "Her sister is pretty, too, don't you think?"

Elizabeth drew in a breath and held it while she waited to hear Will's response. He was slow to answer and seemed to be considering his response as he began to tap his fingers on the table. "I suppose some may consider her pretty… if she is their type."

Charles laughed. "I have yet to discover just who your type is, Will. You baffle me!"

Elizabeth fisted her hands, and as she took a step forward, she heard her phone ring. She saw Will lean over and look at the screen, and then saw him give his head a brisk shake.

Elizabeth hurried over, grabbed the phone from the table, and shot him an accusing glance. "If you don't mind..."

She left and glanced down to see George Wickham had called again.

Jane was at the sink washing her hands when Elizabeth returned to the restroom. "What took you so long?" She looked at Elizabeth. "Is something wrong?"

"I'll tell you about it later." She looked in the mirror at her sister. "Jane, Charles seems delightful, kind, attentive, and everything else you believed him to be." She shook her head. "But his friend!" She paused, and then added, "I feel like he's judging everything I do!"

"Oh, I am certain he is doing no such thing!"

"Well, at least it's just tonight. I can endure his company for another hour or so." She looked at her phone. "George has called twice, so I'm going to text him and let him know you and I are out eating. He keeps asking me to go out with him!"

"I thought you two were just friends."

"So did I, but I guess he didn't get that memo."

Jane smiled. "If you don't mind, I'm going back out."

"And I'll be there in a bit."

Elizabeth sent off a quick text and then turned off the phone so he wouldn't disturb her again.

When she returned to the table, their food was being brought out. She found herself hoping Will would find his steak as good as any he had eaten, but she doubted he would. If he did, he probably wouldn't admit it.

She watched him take his first bite. He seemed bothered about something, as if he had a bad taste in his mouth. She gave her head a slight shake as she realized there would be no pleasing him tonight. Jane and Charles continued to talk, and Elizabeth was content to quietly sit and watch them. Will also seemed content to remain silent.

By the time they had finished their meal, Charles and Jane likely knew everything about each other, while Elizabeth knew nothing more about Will. It was decided they would order one dessert and share it. Cherries jubilee was the one agreed upon. When a song began playing, and a few couples went out onto the dance floor, Charles stood up, extended his hand, and offered it to Jane. "Would you care to dance?"

A smile lit Jane's face. "I would love to."

Elizabeth watched them as they walked away, and then turned to face the only other person at the table. He had also been watching them, and when he turned and met Elizabeth's gaze, she drew back.

"I… uh… No, no. Please don't think you have to ask me to dance. I am not at all inclined to dance."

Will pursed his lips, and then finally said, "I guess that is all good and well because I hadn't intended to ask you to dance."

Elizabeth forced a smile, despite feeling a rather unexpected sense of disappointment. She was at a loss for words, something she rarely experienced. It may have been the intense look in his eyes, but she decided it was that she had no desire to converse with the man sitting across from her.

She turned to watch Charles and Jane as they danced to a slow tune. She felt, rather than saw, Will's eyes were still upon her.

"Look," she said as she turned back to him. "I know neither of us came tonight with any intent – or hope – of it being a date, so we don't have to make a pretense of it."

His eyes narrowed, and then he glanced back at the dancing couple, nodding towards them. "True. I'm quite certain you came to make sure the man your sister met only just yesterday could be trusted." He looked back with a questioning glance. "Correct?"

"You can never be too sure these days."

"Well, I can guarantee you will find no one more kind, respectable, and honorable than Charles."

Elizabeth tilted her head. "And I would guess you are here because Charles asked you to come along because he didn't want me to be a third wheel on his date with Jane." She crossed her arms in front of her on the table. "Am I correct?"

"Not quite."

She widened her eyes. "No?"

"On the contrary. He told me you were accompanying them, and I was the one who asked to join them."

"Why?" She let out a soft laugh. "Were you unable to find a date for tonight?" She regretted saying it the moment it came out of her mouth.

His eyes darkened. It was apparent he did not seem to find any humor in it.

"I wanted to make sure..." He paused and drew in a slow breath. "Charles tends to fall fast and hard for a pretty face. I wanted to make sure Jane was not one of those shallow ladies who is only looking to date a guy with some money, and who will quickly dump him when she has had enough of him."

"Jane would never do that." She shook her head. "Besides, if he has a lot of money, I don't think Jane is even aware of it."

"I'm certain your sister is very sweet, but I also wanted to make sure the woman he claimed to be the answer to all his dreams was not the type of woman who would get hurt when he leaves her behind for another pretty face."

This time Elizabeth lowered her brows. "Are you claiming Charles is a womanizer?"

"Not at all, but he tends to give his heart away too soon, and then discovers too late she may not be everything he thought her to be. At first, there is a spark, then a burst of flames, only to slowly fizzle out." He lowered his brows and added, "Much like the cherries jubilee we'll be having."

Elizabeth's jaw dropped, and she let out a huff. "Do you always meddle in your friend's affairs like this? Do you always have to size up his dates and give him your approval rating?" She paused and lifted a single brow. "Or are you this way with everyone?"

He didn't have the opportunity to reply. The song had ended, and Charles and Jane returned to the table. The waitress followed behind them, bringing four bowls of ice cream to the table.

A chef approached and asked everyone to lean back as he placed the pan of cherries jubilee in the center of the table. When he lit them, they went up in a quick flame that just as quickly diminished.

Jane squealed. "My! That extinguished quickly!"

Will sent Elizabeth a knowing look.

The waitress spooned some of the cherries out onto the mounds of ice cream in front of each of them.

"This looks delicious!" Charles said as he turned to Will. "This is the perfect ending to a perfect dinner! Don't you think?" He glanced back at Jane and smiled.

They all agreed the dessert was superb, and when they had finished, Jane gave Elizabeth a nudge. "I need to go to the restroom. Would you care to join me?"

This was their signal that they needed to talk. She wiped her mouth with her napkin and replied, "Certainly."

When they were inside the restroom, Jane's eyes were bright

and her smile wide. "Oh, Lizzy! I think he is wonderful! Charles invited me to a big Christmas Gala at Will's home coming up in a few weeks. You won't believe where his home is."

"Well, I can't begin to guess, but I assume you are going to tell me."

"It's in Pemberley Estates!"

Elizabeth drew back, surprised. "Really? Those homes are..."

Jane's eyes lit up. "Mansions!" She grasped her sister's hands. "You know how we always wished we could be a little mouse and sneak in through the gates and look around at just one?"

Elizabeth let out a huff. "Well, you can tell me all about it, Jane. When I see what my kids face every day, I'm not sure I care to see how those people live."

"But Lizzy, you are coming, too!"

"Oh, no! I give Charles my hearty approval. You don't need me tagging along on any more of your dates."

"No, you *have* to come. Charles has a business meeting to attend on the other side of town and won't be able to pick me up. He said he could send one of Will's cars for me, but I suggested you and I can just drive over. Or you could invite someone, and he could drive us both over. Like George." She smiled wryly. "Then Charles could bring me home later."

"Oh, Jane, I don't know. But it won't be George."

Jane tilted her head. "You know you want to see it!" She clasped her hands. "Please?"

Elizabeth let out a soft moan. "All right. If I have to..."

Jane squealed and gave her a hug. "Thank you so much! It will be so much fun! You know we will have to buy new dresses for the occasion." She pulled away and then winced. "Oh, and would you mind too much if Charles drove me home tonight? I know you can see he is everything good and honorable."

"Well, I..."

"Please?"

"All right, but I don't want you out later than midnight, or I will call the cops!"

"Thanks, so much!" Jane gave her a mischievous smile. "Don't worry, Momma Lizzy. I'll call you if I won't be home by then."

Chapter 3

When they returned to the table and sat down, Jane turned to Charles. "Elizabeth said she would be more than happy to drive us to the Gala, or she will invite a date who will drive us both, if that is all right."

Charles looked at Jane with a wide grin. "That will be great! I was just telling Will I invited you. It is a pretty big affair." He turned to Will. "Is that okay with you?"

"I see no problem with it."

Elizabeth had to admit she was curious about seeing the inside of a home large enough to host a gala. Most gala events she had been to or heard of were usually held in a large venue made for such things, not a home. "When is it?" she asked.

"On the first Friday in December," Charles replied.

"The first Friday?" Elizabeth opened her phone and pulled up the calendar. "That should work. At first, I thought it was the same day as PREP's Christmas party, but PREP's party is the following week."

"Oh!" exclaimed Jane with a clap of her hands. "PREP's Christmas party is always a big affair. For several years, a company has generously provided a Santa and gifts for all the children."

Elizabeth reached out and placed her hand on her sister's. "Well, probably not this year. I heard from Mr. Forster earlier today. He told me that he has retired, and Forster Electronics has changed ownership. They won't be doing the party this year."

"Oh, no!" Jane exclaimed. "What are you going to do?"

Elizabeth shrugged. "I am not sure, but I will figure out something. I will have one, but this year it will be much simpler."

"That is unfortunate," Jane said. "They always did such a terrific job!"

Elizabeth took a few more bites of her dessert and then stood up. "I hope you don't mind, but I am going to bid you all a good night." She looked at Charles with a smile. "I trust you will get Jane home at a reasonable hour."

Charles laughed and dipped his head. "I will guarantee her safe arrival!"

Will then stood up. "I ought to leave, as well. I have work to do in the morning."

He looked at Elizabeth. "I will walk you out."

"Oh," she said. "Thank you, but there is no need. I am… I am going to stop in the restroom before I leave." She looked at him and Charles. "It was nice meeting you both."

"Same here!" Charles said.

"The pleasure was all mine," Will added.

Elizabeth walked away, wondering if he was being honest. It really was too bad he was so rich. He likely never had to worry about where his next meal would come from, how he was going to buy new clothes, and he certainly had no worries about whether he would ever be evicted from his home. And why did he have to be so handsome? She rolled her eyes at the thought.

She dawdled in the restroom, giving Will more than enough time to leave the restaurant. She came out, said goodnight again to Jane and Charles, and grabbed her coat. She was putting it on and walking towards the front when her heart dropped. Will was standing by the door.

"It's pouring outside. A deluge. I thought I would offer you the use of my umbrella."

"Oh, that isn't..." When he opened the door and she saw how hard the rain was coming down, she thought better of it. "Thank you."

As they walked out, she found herself having to huddle against him to keep from being pelted by the rain. They didn't say much, other than him asking her where her car was. She pointed ahead, and he stayed by her side all the way there. She could smell his cologne and again wished he didn't smell so good.

She pointed to her car, and he walked her to the driver's side, holding the umbrella over her while she opened the door and stepped in. "Thank you. You really didn't have to do this."

"I know."

As he started to walk away, Elizabeth asked, "Where is your

car?"

"It's around the corner over there," he pointed.

She drew in a breath, not really wanting to do what she was about to do, but feeling it was only proper. "There is no sense in you having to walk all that way, when you walked out of your way to take me to my car." She leaned over and unlocked the passenger door. "Hop in, and I'll drive you to your car."

He didn't hesitate to walk around but had to stoop down to get into her small car. He shook off his umbrella before bringing it inside. Elizabeth stifled a laugh as his knees practically hit his chin. "You can adjust the seat if you want." She pointed to the far side of the seat. "It might not help much."

"Thanks." He adjusted the seat, and just as she was about to start the engine, he asked, "Did you always know what you wanted to do?"

"I always wanted to teach, but I had no idea I would be teaching in a tutoring center in Meryton Heights."

"Do you enjoy it?"

She turned to him, surprised. "In a single day I can experience the gamut of emotions. There are rewarding times, such as when a child finally grasps something for the first time, like in math. But there are heartbreaking and difficult times, as well."

"What do you find the most difficult?"

She thought for a moment. "The hardest thing for me is to see some of the families' living conditions. I wish I could do so much more for them. I am not able to help everyone who needs help. Right now, I have a limit of thirty children, and I could easily take another thirty if I had the place and people to help." She looked down at her hands. "And if that was not enough, our center is in the area they plan to bulldoze to put in the parking lot when they build the new convention center."

"Ahh, yes. The city is buying up a lot of land and property there."

She started the engine and pulled out. "At least I have a while to figure out what I will do."

Will was silent until he motioned with his hand. "Turn here. My car is the black one at the end on the right."

When she came to a stop behind his car, instead of getting out, he turned in his seat to look at her. "Do you mind if I ask you something?"

She could barely make out the features on his face, which was only dimly lit by a streetlight above, but she could tell by the tone of his voice he was not particularly pleased about something. "Sure."

"I... When you and Jane went to the restroom the first time, your phone rang. I glanced down, not really intending to look, but I did happen to see the name."

Elizabeth's eyes narrowed. "And?"

"I saw it was from George Wickham."

Elizabeth drew back. "Do you... do you know George Wickham?"

"I do." He turned back in his seat and looked forward. "How well do you know him?"

Elizabeth felt a surge of anger course through her, as though he was interrogating her. "I have known him a few months. We've been on a couple of dates." She noticed him tapping his fingers on the armrest of the door.

Will drew in a breath and let it out slowly. "He isn't a man who can be trusted."

Elizabeth fisted her hands as she took a few moments to calm herself at his audacity. "Look, I think I'm fairly competent to make that judgment on my own."

"Perhaps. You came with your sister tonight to make sure Charles was a decent guy. I have been debating all night whether to say anything to you, especially after you accused me of meddling in my friend's affairs, but I can't be silent, especially..."

Elizabeth tilted her head. "Especially... what?"

"Look... You are certainly welcome to invite someone to the Gala, but I don't think it would be wise for you to ask him. It might not be a pretty scene between us if he showed up."

Elizabeth faced forward, and her fingers gripped the steering wheel as anger surged through her. She took a few deep breaths and turned back to him.

"Will Darcy, you may be CEO of a large corporation and are used to telling your employees what they can and can't do. You have every right to. You do not, however, have the right to tell me – or even your friend – what you think we should or shouldn't do, who we should or shouldn't date. I am certain we are both perfectly capable of making sound judgments without your interference."

She looked ahead at Will's car, realizing it was a luxury car that likely cost more than a house. Thoughts and accusations swirled in her head, but she said nothing. Finally, she whispered, "I think this conversation is over."

He opened the door, but before getting out, he turned back to her. "Elizabeth, it was not my intention to offend you or question your judgment. I am sorry if I did."

Elizabeth pursed her lips and let out a quick breath.

He turned and opened his umbrella, but then looked back. "Good night, Elizabeth. I'll see you at the Gala."

Elizabeth only murmured an affirmative. He stepped out of the car, and Elizabeth watched as he hurried over to his and got in. "I suppose if he lives in Pemberley Estates, it would be expected for him to drive a car like that."

She shook her head and pulled away, seething at his meddling in people's lives. While she had decided that George was not her type, she had always found him to be kind and polite. Her biggest issue with him was that he didn't seem to get the hint she didn't want to date him. She wondered just what it was Will had against him. She pounded the steering wheel with her fist. "The nerve of that man! I have never met anyone like him!"

~~*

Will drove away a little faster than he should have, especially considering how slick the streets were. He was grateful for the stability control system his car had, but he still needed to slow down and be careful. He took in a few breaths to calm himself and shook his head. As another car sped past him, he realized he needed to be watching out for other drivers, as well.

"I shouldn't be this upset," he reprimanded himself. He stopped at a red light and listened to the rain pelting the windshield, feeling pelted himself with prickles of frustration. He began to rub his jaw. Was it Elizabeth Bennet or George Wickham that had him most upset? Or both? He couldn't decide. When the light turned green, he put both hands on the steering wheel, began tapping it with his fingers, and slowly pulled ahead.

She had gotten under his skin from the moment she had uttered, '*Snobs* on the Hill.' He was aware of the reputation the elite restaurant had, and at times, he agreed, despite it being unsurpassed in food, service, and atmosphere. At their first encounter outside the restaurant when she had uttered the name – or the derogatory nickname – of Hobbs on the Hill, he had suspected this young lady was either Jane or her sister, as he had been the one who suggested to Charles they go there.

At that first moment he had the fleeting thought – no, in truth, it was hope – that she wasn't Jane. He found himself unwittingly attracted to her. When he had stepped inside behind her and saw Charles sitting with another lady, he felt that hope surge. He was delighted that she turned out to be her sister, Elizabeth, but at the same time was rather dismayed at her seemingly instant dislike of him.

What was it? Was it something he did or said? Was there something about his personality she disliked? He knew what had prompted her dislike of him to intensify at the end of the evening, but there seemed to be something bothering her about him from the very start.

He shrugged. He might never know, but there was the Christmas Gala that she would be attending with her sister. Perhaps he could remedy whatever it was that she found so distasteful about him. Or, then again, it could end up being just another one of those instances where a woman he found attractive would slip through his fingers.

He could still vividly see her delightful face, but especially her eyes. They were sharp, bright, and intelligent. They laughed and derided, teased and rebuked. But when she spoke of her dreams for the tutoring center, they were filled with such passion. He could see that she loved what she did and loved the children. He truly felt if anyone could accomplish those lofty goals, she could.

She was different, and he liked that. He had not met anyone quite like her. He let out a mocking laugh. "I find a woman undeniably desirable, and she despises me." He pounded the steering wheel. "Yes, she is refreshingly different!"

He could help her. He knew he could help her and the daycare – the tutoring center – but he wouldn't want her to feel any sense of indebtedness towards him. She didn't want his help, and he didn't want to buy her affections. But he could still help her.

He pulled into a long driveway and entered his code at the gate. As he waited for the wide gates to open, he tapped his fingers again on the steering wheel. He pulled through and drove into the garage.

He turned off the engine and pulled out his phone, pressing the button to call his cousin.

"Hello?" the voice answered on the other end.

"Hey, Richard, are you busy?"

"No, Will, what's up?"

"I have something I would like you to do for me." He paused. "And you're probably going to laugh when I tell you what it is, but I am serious."

When they finished talking – or at least, when he finished talking Richard into his scheme – he got out of the car, feeling a great sense of satisfaction.

Chapter 4

When Jane came home a few minutes after midnight, she lightly tapped on Elizabeth's bedroom door, and then quietly opened it.

"Are you awake, Lizzy?"

Elizabeth stirred and slowly lifted her head. "I am now."

"I'm sorry."

Elizabeth waved her in and then patted the bed. "Come, sit down, and tell me how the rest of your evening with Charles was." She sat up, took her pillow, and fluffed it up, propping it up behind her. "Now that I'm comfortable, I am ready to hear all about it!"

Jane hurried over and sat down. "Oh, Lizzy! He is wonderful! He's exactly the kind of man a girl wants." She giggled. "At least the kind of guy that *I* want." She leaned in. "What did you think of him?"

"Well, I thought he was very handsome, kind, and friendly." She tilted her head. "What did you do after we... after I left?"

"We danced a few more dances, and talked, and then we just drove around. It had stopped raining by then." She let out a laugh. "He took me to an antique mall that stays open until midnight on Fridays and Saturdays. We walked around looking at fun things."

Elizabeth smiled. "Did either of you buy anything?"

Jane shook her head. "No. We were enjoying each other's company so much that we hardly noticed all the things for sale around us."

"He is sweet."

Jane looked down. "Yes, he is." She lifted her eyes to her sister. "But I wish you had liked Will. Charles seems to think highly of him. He has known him a long time."

Elizabeth's eyes narrowed as she pondered this. "The two of them are quite different. Will is... I don't know. I guess I see him as a typical wealthy CEO who puts work and money in front of everything, and..." She paused.

"And what?"

"There were some things he said that made me think he is also the type who wants to control those around him."

"Do you mean Charles?"

Elizabeth reached out for Jane's hands. "He did say he came to make sure Charles was not falling for some shallow girl who was not good enough for him."

Jane let out a laugh. "Elizabeth, you do realize that is the very same reason you wanted to come along with me!"

"No, no..." Her voice trailed off. "Well, that's different." She tilted her head and looked at Jane. "There were other things he said when he walked me to my car."

Jane drew back in surprise. "He walked you to your car? I thought by the time you left, he would have been long gone!"

Elizabeth shrugged. "Me too! I was surprised to see him still there. He waited for me because it was pouring outside, and he knew I didn't have an umbrella."

"Did he? I find that rather gentlemanly. Not many men would have done that."

"Now, Jane, don't go getting any ideas about how heroic he is. There is a side to him that rubs me the wrong way."

Jane extended her arm and placed her hand on her sister's shoulder. "It's the money, isn't it?"

"No, it's not just that." She let out a chuckle. "Although, he is a man who drives a luxury car, prefers to go to upscale restaurants, and..."

"Lives in Pemberley Estates!" they both said at the same time, followed by a shared laugh.

"I don't know. I guess I'm feeling a lot of stress right now about PREP and what is to become of it. I'm not even looking forward to Christmas because we can't do the party like we've always done."

"Will you still be able to have the party?"

"Oh, we'll have one. We'll make ornaments and have Christmas goodies and sing songs, but there will be no presents and no Santa to hand them out like we've had the past few years." She leaned her head back and rubbed her neck. "The kids have been so looking forward to it, but how can I expect to find someone willing to donate all those gifts at the last minute?"

Jane leaned over and kissed her sister on her cheek. "The kids will appreciate anything you do for them." Jane clasped her hands. "It's late. It's been an amazing evening, and I'm going to bed."

Elizabeth reached out and squeezed her sister's hand. "Sweet dreams, Jane."

"You, too!" Jane stood up and walked to the door, turning back with a smile. "I know I will!"

~~*

A week before the Christmas Gala, Jane finally convinced Elizabeth that they needed to go shopping for dresses. Elizabeth had been putting it off all week, as she was not really in a Christmas mood. Before setting out to go shopping, Elizabeth's phone rang.

She picked up her phone and looked at it. Not recognizing the number and seeing no name, she debated whether to just let it go to voicemail. Something inside of her, however, nudged her to answer.

"Hello?"

A pleasant-sounding woman on the other end replied, "Hello. This is Mrs. Evans from F&D Consultants. Is this Elizabeth Bennet?"

"Yes, it is."

"Do you have a few minutes? I have something I would like to discuss with you. I think you will be quite pleased."

Elizabeth readied herself for some marketing ploy, but as she listened to Mrs. Evans give her reasons for calling, her eyes widened, her jaw dropped, and her heart began to soar.

When the call ended, Elizabeth called out to her sister. "Jane! Come here! You won't believe what just happened!"

Jane came out brushing her long, blond hair. "What is it?"

"I just received a call from a woman at F&D Company or Consultants, or something like that, and they would like to supply all the presents for our Christmas party, as well as have someone dressed as Santa come deliver them!"

Jane rushed over to her sister and wrapped her arms about her. "Elizabeth! That is wonderful news! I knew things would work out!"

"You are always the optimist! I confess I really doubted

whether it would happen."

"How did they come to hear about your need?"

"The woman who called didn't know all the details, but she said someone from their company had been talking to Mr. Forster or knew him and found out his company was no longer able to put on the party. She said their company is always looking for ways to help organizations that directly meet people's needs in the city."

"It sounds like a wonderful company!"

Elizabeth nodded enthusiastically. "Yes, it does!" She leaned over and gave Jane a kiss on her cheek. "For some odd reason, now I am excited about going out and buying a dress for the Gala and…" She wore a wide smile. "I am actually excited about the Gala itself!"

Jane returned her smile. "That makes me so happy!"

"When we finish, I have got a lot of work to do!"

Jane looked confused. "But what do you have to do if this company is putting on the party?"

"I need to make a list of my kids, their ages, and some suggestions of things to buy for them."

"Wow! I assumed they would just get all the kids the same thing! This is great!"

"I know," Elizabeth said as tears filled her eyes. "I really can't believe this is happening!"

~~*

Neither Jane nor Elizabeth had any idea what they were looking for in a dress, but Jane knew she would know it when she saw it. Elizabeth only knew that whatever she bought today would likely never be worn again. She could count on one finger how many formal events she had ever attended, and it was her high school prom.

They decided to go to a large department store first.

"I have no idea what to even look for, Jane," Elizabeth said as they walked through the store. "I can only remember how stressful it was when I went looking for my prom dress." She laughed and stole a glance at her sister. "Do you remember?"

Jane touched her sister's shoulder. "Of course! But you do remember why it was so stressful, don't you?"

They both smiled and replied together, "Mother!"

After a laugh, Elizabeth said, "Oh, she was impossible! She would not give her approval of anything that showed any shoulder, back, or... or..."

"I think she would have only been happy with a potato sack!" Jane said with a chuckle. She gave her a reassuring smile. "It is just us, today, and I will give my hearty approval of anything you like."

Elizabeth reached up and clasped Jane's hand. "And I will do the same for you."

They walked through the toiletries department, and Elizabeth stopped. "What is that smell?"

"Probably a man's aftershave," Jane replied.

"May I help you?" the store associate asked.

"Is that a man's cologne I smell?"

The woman smiled. "Yes! A lady was just here sampling several different brands, but she found this cologne to be very pleasant." She held it towards them. "Give me your wrist and I will spritz a little on to see if this is what you smell."

Elizabeth complied, and she lifted it to her nose. "Yes, this is it. Can you tell me what it is?"

"It is a fairly new cologne, called Ardently."

"That smells familiar," Jane said. "I have smelled it before."

"Would you care to buy some for your boyfriend?" she directed her question to Elizabeth.

"No, he already..." She paused, giving her head a shake. "No, thank you. Not today."

As they walked away, Jane smiled. "Will was wearing that at the restaurant, wasn't he?"

Elizabeth gave a harrumph. "I have no idea!" She was grateful Jane said no more about it as they walked away.

They had no luck finding anything in the selection of formal dresses at the department store, so decided to try Elite Boutique, a second-hand store that carried formal and casual dresses at reasonable prices.

They entered the store, and as they walked around looking at dresses, one would comment on the deep, rich color, but didn't like the style. Or they loved the style but weren't crazy about the color.

"What do you think of this one?" Elizabeth asked as she held up a berry red dress.

"It's a great Christmas color. You can wear such bright colors, whereas when I do, they just make me look pale and more washed out than I already am." Jane tapped her finger on her chin.

"Why don't you try it on?"

Elizabeth smiled. "I think I will."

When she put it on and stepped out of the dressing room, Jane placed a hand over her mouth. Her eyes widened, and she exclaimed, "Lizzy, it looks stunning on you!"

Elizabeth walked over to a mirror and stood back, turning around as she studied her reflection. "You don't think it is too tight… or the neckline is too low?"

"It is very flattering. You have the figure to fill out a dress like that." Jane looked down at herself. "I only wish I did."

As Elizabeth continued to turn around and look at herself at every angle, Jane continued to look through the dresses, occasionally pulling one out and asking her sister what she thought. She finally pulled out a pale green dress. "What do you think of this one?"

Elizabeth came over and gave her sister a nod. "It matches your eyes, Jane. I think this one could be it." She suddenly laughed. "Wouldn't it be nice to buy both dresses here?"

"It would. I think I'll go try it on."

Elizabeth handed her dress to the saleswoman and continued to look around just in case she found something she liked better. When Jane stepped out, Elizabeth hurried over to her. "Jane, oh, Jane. You look like an angel. I love the flowing skirt."

"You really like it?"

"I do. What do you think? That's what's important."

Jane walked over to the mirror and sighed as she gazed at her reflection. "I like it, but it's probably because it is the prettiest dress I've ever worn." She gave a slight shrug. "I think this is the one."

"Then I think you should get it. The prettiest dress for the prettiest young lady at the Gala. I can guarantee that Charles won't be able to take his eyes off you."

"Are you getting the red one?"

Elizabeth nodded and laughed. "I am! I'm so glad we are both easy to please."

While Jane slipped out of her dress and put her clothes back on, Elizabeth found a pair of earrings just the right color, adding it to her order.

After paying for their purchases and walking out of the store, Elizabeth asked, "Now we have the rest of the day to do as we please. What would you like to do?"

"How about getting something to eat? Looking at all those dresses made me hungry."

Elizabeth laughed, feeling like she was much more in the Christmas spirit than she had been just the day before. "That sounds like a good idea."

Chapter 5

On the evening of the Christmas Gala, Elizabeth and Jane spent a good amount of time getting ready. Afterwards, they drove to their parents' home to show them their new gowns.

When they walked in, their mother, Frances Bennet, gushed about how lovely they looked.

Tom Bennet looked up from his book and let out a whistle. "You two girls always look pretty."

Frances, however, showered the girls with advice on how to act. "There will be a lot of wealthy, important people there. You must pay attention to all you say and do, walk gracefully, and hold your heads up high. Whatever you do, don't offend Charles or the hosts."

"Yes, Mother," both girls replied.

Tom stood up and pulled out his phone. "Let me get a picture of the two of you." He waved his hand. "Go stand in front of the tree. You both look so... Christmassy!"

"That's a great idea!" Elizabeth said, as she and Jane walked over to the tree. They smiled as their father took several pictures.

"I'll let you look at these later and you can pick out any that you want."

"Thanks!" They both replied.

"Oh!" Tom said. "I forgot something." He held out a set of keys.

"What is this?" Elizabeth asked.

"You may want to take my car. I went into Pemberley Estates years ago when I was a telephone repairman, and well..." He shook his head. "You know how some restaurants have dress codes?"

Elizabeth and Jane nodded.

"Well, I wouldn't be surprised if Pemberley Estates has a car code." He slowly shook his head. "I don't think your little car will pass muster."

"Oh, Dad, I'm sure they don't..."

Tom's eyes twinkled, and he let out a laugh. "No, I'm sure they don't. And my car isn't that fancy, either. But I think you will feel more comfortable in a larger car than in your little puddle jumper."

Elizabeth reached out and took the keys. "Thanks."

"No need to bring it back tonight. Just return it at your leisure tomorrow."

"Great!" Elizabeth drew in a deep breath. "Well, I guess it's time to go." She turned to Jane. "Are you ready?"

"I've been ready for quite some time."

"Good! Let's go!"

They kissed their parents goodnight, and as they walked out the door, they heard their mother call out to them.

"Don't forget to smile and be on your best behavior!"

Elizabeth let out a frustrated sigh. "Yes, Mother." She paused and then laughed. "How have we survived all these years?"

Jane shrugged and shook her head.

"What does she think we are going to do?"

Jane let out a soft sigh. "I don't know, but I sometimes wonder if Charles will suddenly think I'm not good enough for him, or I might do something wrong or say the wrong thing."

Elizabeth took her sister's hand. "You could never say or do anything wrong. Charles is a wonderful man who adores you." She glanced down at their hands. "When do you plan on bringing him over to meet our parents?"

Jane turned back and looked at their home. "He plans to join us on Christmas Day. He'll be spending the morning with his family and will be coming by in the afternoon."

Elizabeth smiled at Jane, but inwardly, she hoped that Charles was wonderful enough to ignore the idiosyncrasies of their family. In addition to their mother, they had three younger sisters – triplets, actually – Mary, Kitty, and Lydia, who were presently all away at college. Mary was attending a small Bible college up north, and Kitty and Lydia were enrolled in a state college about two hours away. Despite being triplets, they were very different from each other, as well as from Jane and herself. Elizabeth often wondered how they could all have the same parents.

"We'll just have to tell everyone to be on their best behavior!" Elizabeth said with a laugh.

Jane stole a glance at her sister. "Is that even possible?"

Elizabeth shrugged. "I have no idea, but it's worth a try!"

~~*

When they reached the gated community of Pemberley Estates, several cars were in line ahead of them, as visitors had to stop at the booth before being allowed to enter. Other cars drove past them through the lane that allowed residents to enter by way of a sensor that opened a separate gate. Jane opened her purse and pulled out a hand-drawn map Charles had made for her.

"This should help us find it," she said. "He said their home is difficult to find with all the winding streets up here." She glanced out the window. "Especially when it's dark."

Elizabeth reached for her phone and handed it to Jane. "I think it will be easier to use GPS."

Jane took the phone and entered the address written on the paper. She then folded up the paper and placed it back in her purse.

"Looking at all the other cars in line, I am beginning to wonder if Dad was right about the car code." Elizabeth turned to Jane with a smile. "Most of these are luxury cars."

"I'm glad he gave us his to drive." Jane rubbed her hand across the seat. "It may be old and doesn't have all the fancy gadgets new cars have now, but it is nice."

Elizabeth rolled down her window as they approached the booth.

"Good evening," said the young man inside. "Who are you visiting tonight?"

"We are going to the Christmas Gala at the Darcy home."

"And your name?"

"Bennet. Elizabeth and Jane Bennet."

He looked down at a list and then nodded. "Ah, yes, here you are. Do you know your way to the home?"

"Not exactly, but we have a hand drawn map and GPS on our phone."

"Well, it might be just as easy to follow those three cars ahead of you. That's where they're heading." He smiled at Elizabeth. "The area is pretty hilly with many curves and side streets."

Elizabeth smiled. "Thanks! I think following them will be a lot easier."

The young man handed them a card. "Place this inside your front windshield on the passenger side."

Elizabeth reached out and took it, and then handed it to Jane. "Thanks again, and... Merry Christmas."

The young man laughed. "Same to you. Enjoy your evening."

Elizabeth drove a little faster than the posted speed limit so she could catch up to the cars ahead of her, and she was grateful when the last car was in view.

"This is much better. Instead of looking down at a map, I can keep my eyes on the road – and the scenery. It's a very nice area, but all the mansions!" Elizabeth pointed out her side of the window. "Look at that one! I think it is a little too extravagant."

"I can't imagine living in a place like that," Jane said. "And look at that one! Oh, my!"

Elizabeth shook her head slowly. "Will probably has one of those cold modern homes with very little furniture in the rooms."

Jane let out a soft huff. "Elizabeth, I don't know why you are so antagonistic towards him. I thought he was very handsome, gentlemanly, and…" She shrugged. "So what if he is rich?"

Elizabeth kept her eyes on the road and let out a groan.

"I do have my suspicions," Jane said with a conspiratorial smile.

"Oh, do you?" Elizabeth said.

"You're attracted to him and are doing everything in your power to convince yourself he isn't right for you just because he's wealthy."

"Oh, really, Jane. Attracted to him? I think not."

"Lizzy, not everyone who has money is like the Gouldings."

Elizabeth rolled her eyes. "I know, but money does make people behave differently, and they're often only looking out for themselves. People who are driven to make a lot of money tend to have that as their main passion in life." She tightened her grip on the steering wheel.

"Perhaps Will is different."

A look of doubt spread across Elizabeth's face. She gave a small shrug.

"Whatever your reasons for not liking Will, just be polite to him tonight."

Elizabeth looked over at her sister and smiled. "Yes, Mother!" Both girls laughed.

They continued up the winding road, commenting on many of the immense homes. Most had outdoor lighting that lit up the front, as well as those with Christmas lights that made them easy to see. The car ahead soon took a right turn, and Elizabeth did the same.

"I bet we're getting close," Elizabeth said. She pointed to the right. "I think I see some decorations up ahead."

The cars began to slow down, and Elizabeth leaned her head to the side to see what was happening. "It looks like they have valet parking." She slapped her hands on the steering wheel. "Now I'm glad Dad lent us his car!" She stopped and suddenly pointed. "Look!" It barely came out in a whisper.

Off to the side was a beautiful home that looked like it had been modeled after an English country manor. It was tastefully beautiful, not extraordinarily opulent or modern, but very pleasing to the eye. It was a two-story stone and wood structure with a large picture window displaying a festive Christmas tree inside. A small pond in front of the home reflected the array of colored and blinking lights on the house.

Jane's jaw dropped. "Oh, my! It is lovely!"

"It's not only lovely, but also charming, beautiful, and very inviting!" Elizabeth looked at her sister, and they both smiled.

A valet drove away in the car ahead of them, and then Elizabeth was waved forward.

She pulled up and stopped, and when their doors were opened, she and Jane stepped out. Jane started to hum along with the Christmas music they heard. Elizabeth took the card the valet handed her and placed it in her purse. She wrapped her coat tightly about her and hurried to her sister's side, as they took the long stone pathway to the house.

"Do you think Will decorates the whole house?" Jane asked.

Elizabeth let out a huff. "I am certain he hires a decorating company to come decorate everything. He probably doesn't want anything to do with it."

Jane shrugged. "I suppose. He probably doesn't have the time to do it."

Elizabeth pointed ahead. "Look! There is a small orchestra and carolers!" A wide smile appeared. "Look at how they're dressed!"

They stopped and listened to the quartet sing. The two ladies wore long red dresses that were flared at the bottom and had red and black plaid shawls edged with white fur that cradled their heads like a hood. The two men wore black pants, coats, and top hats, and had plaid scarves that matched the ladies' shawls. They each held a black music folder, and an old-fashioned lamplight shone down on them from behind.

A small crowd gathered and listened appreciatively as the carolers sang *Carol of the Bells*.

Elizabeth found herself swaying to the lively tune. When it was over, the small crowd clapped and began to walk inside. Elizabeth and Jane walked up to the carolers.

"That was beautiful, and it isn't an easy song to sing." She turned and addressed the instrumentalists in the eight-piece orchestra. "Or an easy song to play. We enjoyed it immensely."

They were appreciative of her words and began playing their next song.

"Well," Elizabeth said as she took Jane's arm. "As much as I would prefer to stay out here and listen to the music, I suppose we should go in. Shall we?"

Jane's face lit up in a smile. "I can't wait!"

Elizabeth and Jane walked towards the intricately carved double wooden front doors. Small white blinking lights bounced off the leaded crystal windows on either side of the doors. A young man standing in front of the door greeted them and asked for their names. When Elizabeth gave them to him, he looked down at the clipboard he held, perusing the list. When he found their names, he smiled, checked them off, and opened the door, ushering them in.

"If you will proceed to the left, you can check your coats and any other items you don't want to carry with you. You will then find the family gathered to greet the guests just down the hall on the right."

"Thank you," Elizabeth and Jane said together.

They checked their coats and purses and stepped into a wide entryway that was strung with garlands of greens, red berries, red plaid bows, and tiny white lights. The music being played outdoors echoed softly into the open space. Up ahead, Elizabeth spotted the tree she had seen in the window, decorated with glistening bulbs and twinkling lights.

The alluring scent of pine wafted through the air. Whether it was from the candles that were burning, diffusing essential oils, or the tree itself, Elizabeth was not certain, but she felt as though she had just stepped into a Christmas wonderland.

As they followed the crowd, her gaze lingered on the tree ahead of them. She didn't think she had ever seen such a tall, full tree inside a home. The vaulted ceiling allowed for the tree to rise in stately prominence, completely unobstructed.

Jane stopped, looking about her. Her eyes were wide and dancing with delight. "Isn't it beautiful?"

She looked intently at her sister. "Have you ever seen anything so beautiful?"

Elizabeth let out a laugh. "Hardly! But I'm sure the company that decorated the house was paid a pretty penny to do only the best." She shook her head. "They certainly have an array of beautiful decorations giving it the perfect Christmas feeling."

They heard a familiar voice call out, and they both turned to see Charles, hurrying towards them.

"I am so glad you made it," he said. "Did you find the house okay?"

"Yes! Your map helped immensely!" Jane answered, giving a sly, knowing look to her sister.

Charles turned to Elizabeth. "Thank you so much for bringing Jane. I had to rush home and change after my meeting, and I had no idea how traffic was going to be, especially coming from the other side of town."

"It was my pleasure," she said.

Elizabeth turned back, and she could now see Will standing a few feet away. He looked up and his eyes locked with hers. There was an intensity about them that made her shiver. Was he upset she had come? He knew she would be there, but would he have preferred not to see her again?

Elizabeth noticed others standing alongside him who also greeted the guests. There was an older woman, with silver hair wrapped in a bun in the back of her head. She had grey eyes that crinkled when she smiled, and an ivory complexion touched with a few wrinkles that added a touch of warmth and wisdom to her features. Between them was a girl with blond hair and fair skin, who reached Will's shoulders in height.

The party ahead of them moved on and began conversing with another couple standing just beyond Will and the two ladies.

Will turned and looked at her. "Good evening, Elizabeth and Jane. I see you made it, Charles. I am glad you have all come. Let me introduce you to my family."

Will made the introductions. The older woman turned out to be Will's grandmother, Evelyn Darcy. The young girl was his sixteen-year-old sister, Georgiana.

"Is this your first time attending the Christmas Gala?" Georgiana asked.

"Yes, it is," Elizabeth answered. "It's the first time I've come to anything like this!"

"We are delighted to be here, "Jane added.

The older woman extended a thin, frail hand and grasped Elizabeth's. "Thank you for coming, my dears. I hope you will enjoy yourselves."

"Thank you," Elizabeth said. "I'm sure we will."

Will pointed ahead. "If you just follow the line of people, you will find refreshments in the room straight ahead and a sealed bid auction in the room on the left. The proceeds for that auction go to several charities that you will find listed in the room." He nodded at his friend. "Charles knows his way around and can direct you." He then looked at Elizabeth. "If you walk further down the hall and veer to the right, there is a room where there will be music and dancing a little later."

As he said this, Elizabeth wondered if he was thinking of their comments to each other about not wanting to dance when they had first met.

"Thank you," Elizabeth said, as the party ahead of them moved on.

"And please, allow me to introduce you to my aunt and uncle."

The couple standing on the other side of Will's grandmother was her daughter and son-in-law.

After speaking briefly with the couple, they walked away. Charles leaned in and said quietly, "Will's parents died in a car accident about four years ago. Will was suddenly thrust into the position of CEO of the family company and guardian to his sister."

"That is so sad," Jane said.

"It really is," Elizabeth said as she turned back and saw Will's eyes on her again. She drew in an unsteady breath and quickly turned back. "Everything's so beautiful! I love all the Christmas decorations."

"That is what Darcy Enterprises specializes in. Years ago, his grandparents began going overseas to Christmas markets and importing decorations back to the states. His mother continued doing it until she died, and now his aunt oversees several people who scour the world for the most unique and beautiful Christmas decorations, in addition to gifts and home decor."

Jane's eyes lit up. "It must be Christmas all year round here!"

Charles laughed. "Just about. Now, would you like to get some refreshments or check out the items in the auction?"

"I think I'd like something to drink," Jane said.

As they walked down the long hallway, they passed a room that caught Elizabeth's attention. "Look, Jane! A library!" She peered in and drew in a quick breath. "It's beautiful!"

Charles smiled. "Will is certainly a reader! His whole family is. Me on the other hand, not so much. He has always encouraged me to read more, but I always had a difficult time slogging through the reading I was required to do!"

Jane nodded to her sister. "Lizzy would be in heaven there! She and my father are avid readers!"

They came to the large room at the end of the hallway filled with long tables laden with drinks and a grand selection of foods. Charles picked up some goblets of sparkling wine for himself and the ladies.

They were talking and enjoying their refreshments when a shrill voice drew their attention.

"Charles! There you are!"

Jane and Elizabeth watched as a tall, slender woman rushed up to them. She was wearing a low-cut beaded gown, as well as a diamond-studded necklace, earrings, and a dangling bracelet.

"So, is this Jane, whom I have heard so much about?" She stretched out her arms and took Jane's hands in hers.

"Indeed, it is! Jane, I would like you to meet my sister, Caroline. Caroline, this is Jane Bennet, and her sister, Elizabeth."

Chapter 6

"It is a delight to finally meet you," Caroline said to Jane. She looked at Elizabeth. "And you."

"Thank you. It's a pleasure to meet you," Jane replied.

Elizabeth smiled and nodded.

Charles clasped his hands together. "You ladies can get acquainted while I get us some appetizers."

Caroline released Jane's hands and drew back, tilting her head. "Such charming dresses! Who is the designer? Where did you purchase them?"

Jane looked a little confused, while Elizabeth did her best to not roll her eyes.

Elizabeth leaned in as if to confide in her, and with a confident, yet challenging smile, answered, "Elite Boutique on Market Street."

Caroline tilted her head slightly. "Oh, I see. I don't recall ever hearing of it, but they are both… charming dresses." She glanced down at hers. "This is a Marlina original. I'm sure you've heard of her. She has a shop just a few miles from here." She glanced up and seemed to focus on something – or someone – behind them. "Only the best for the Darcy Christmas Gala."

She took Jane's hand again. "I'm delighted to have finally met you. I have heard so much about you. We shall have to meet for lunch soon."

Caroline suddenly turned her head as a couple walked by. "Oh, Paul and Lilly! It has been far too long! How was your trip to the French Riviera?"

"It was lovely," the woman replied. "We have decided we must return again in the near future!" She turned to Elizabeth and Jane. "Are these friends of yours?"

"Oh, these are just some friends of Charles. Jane and Elizabeth… I am sorry, I can't recall your last name."

"Bennet," the sisters replied.

"It is nice to meet you," Lilly said. "Is this your first Gala?"

"Yes, it is," Jane replied.

"Well, I hope you enjoy it. We have been coming for at least ten years and would never miss it."

Caroline turned as she tucked her hand in Lilly's arm. "Now, you must tell me all about your trip." The threesome walked away.

Shortly after, Charles returned with a plate filled with cookies, cakes, and sweets, and as they enjoyed them, he introduced them to several acquaintances of his.

Elizabeth was pleased that most of the people they met were not at all like Caroline Bingley, and she was able to engage many in conversation about her tutoring program. She enjoyed talking about it, and many seemed interested in hearing her dreams and vision for it.

Later, as Charles and Jane began conversing between themselves, Elizabeth found herself looking about the room. She told herself she was not watching for Will to walk in, but if she were honest with herself, that was who she was looking for.

When Charles began talking to another acquaintance, Elizabeth turned to Jane and whispered, "If you do not mind, I am going to go check out the auction."

"I hope you find something. Charles and I may join you in a bit."

Elizabeth turned and walked back down the long hallway. She stepped into the room where the auction was being held and glanced at the poster listing all the charities the monies would go towards. She was impressed that there was such a variety of well-known charitable organizations and some she had never heard of.

Elizabeth turned back and looked at the array of items set out on tables and muttered to herself, "Where do I begin?"

"Wherever you want."

She turned to see Evelyn Darcy standing there.

"Oh, Mrs. Darcy, please allow me to tell you how beautiful everything looks. I understand Darcy Enterprises imports Christmas decorations from around the world."

"Thank you, my dear. I am so glad you appreciate them. Each year it is a labor of love to decorate."

"I am sure it is! And all the items in the auction! This is quite the selection."

"It is," she replied.

Elizabeth smiled at the older woman. "Can you please tell me how the bidding works?"

"I would be delighted to explain. It is a sealed bid auction, so people have no idea what the other bids are or even how many there are. You put your name and phone number on the paper and the amount you are willing to pay and place it in the box by the item. There is a minimum bid by each of the items, and you can bid that amount, if you choose. If no one else bids on it, it is yours. Once the auction is closed, the one with the highest bid wins."

"I like that," Elizabeth said. "I have been to auctions where you have a running bid on a sheet of paper, and when it comes close to ending, people are gathered around trying to be the final, highest bidder."

Mrs. Darcy laughed. "That is exactly why my husband chose to do it this way. He didn't like the greed and disrespect that was often displayed." She tilted her head. "He had been to auctions where they had to break up a fight when several people were vying to be the final, winning bid!"

Elizabeth's jaw dropped. "A fight? Really?"

"It wasn't here, but when he witnessed it elsewhere, he decided we were going to do our auctions this way to take away that whole element. Hopefully, people will bid what they feel they can afford, and not be pressured to keep raising it to a higher amount."

"That is very wise," Elizabeth said reflectively. "How long have you been putting on the Christmas Gala?"

"This is our thirty-seventh year." She smiled and leaned towards Elizabeth with a conspiratorial smile. "Don't tell him I told you this, but when Will was just four years old, he came to the Gala for the first time. Everyone thought he looked so cute in his red and green Christmas outfit, but he soon had enough of everyone pinching his cheeks and gushing over him, that he disappeared, and no one could find him."

Elizabeth laughed. "Where was he?"

"He hid under one of the auction tables. With the long table skirts, no one saw him, and he fell asleep under there."

Elizabeth smiled at the image of that little boy. "Where do all the items come from?"

"They're all donated, either from individuals or corporations. It is amazing what people are willing to give for the benefit of a charity." She paused and then asked, "Is there anything else you would like to know or anything in particular you are looking for?"

"I think I am just going to browse, thank you." She began to walk away and then stopped. "I hope you don't mind my asking, but I noticed your necklace when we came in. I have never seen anything like it. The pendant is quite unusual, but beautiful. May I ask what it is?"

Evelyn Darcy fingered the piece around her neck. "No, I don't mind at all! It belonged to my mother, and this frosted piece in the center of the pendant is called camphor glass."

Elizabeth looked up. "I have never heard of it."

"Camphor glass was a material used in jewelry in the twenties and thirties. I always liked the filigree silver and gold design on it and the tiny diamonds." She let out a soft chuckle. "It isn't as ostentatious as so many people wear these days. My father gave it to my mother for her wedding gift, as they were married in December." She leaned in. "He told her it reminded him of a frosted windowpane."

"Ah! I can certainly see why!" Elizabeth said with a smile.

"They didn't have a lot of money back then. She always wore it at Christmastime." She smiled, and was silent for a moment, as if lost in thought. "I wore it for my December wedding, and I still do, as often as I can, around Christmas. It isn't worth very much, but it has a lot of sentimental value to me."

"I can certainly see why. It is beautiful."

"Thank you, my dear."

Elizabeth thanked her for her help and began to walk around the room. She let out a small gasp when she saw the variety of things being auctioned off. She walked past a weekend stay at a bed and breakfast, two prime seats for the symphony, a big screen television, and a diamond necklace set with earrings and bracelet. She leaned in closer and shook her head, thinking it was beautiful, but not in her budget.

The items all had a description of what it was, who donated it, and the minimum bid.

From across the room, she noticed some computers and immediately walked over to them. There were five laptop models with the latest programs, video and editing software, speakers and headphones included. There was also a 5-year warranty. She looked at the minimum bid and then noticed Will had donated them.

"I wish it hadn't been him," she said softly to herself with a shrug. "Well, chances are he won't even know I bid on them, and it is even more unlikely I will win the bid."

She had been saving up to buy some computers to begin a computer lab at the school and reasoned that she could afford to bid the minimum bid – or a little higher. It would certainly be a bargain if she were to have the winning bid, but it would also be a miracle.

She filled out the bidding form with her name and phone number and then, drawing in a long breath, she wrote down an amount she hoped would be enough above the minimum bid to win. She folded her bid, tucked it into a small envelope, and then dropped it into the box.

"There! Now all I have to do is hope and pray – for a miracle!"

She walked around and found a few more things that she was tempted to bid on for herself but refrained. She noticed Jane and Charles had come in, and they were placing a bid in a box.

"And what are you bidding on?" Elizabeth asked as she walked up to them.

Jane answered. "Two season tickets to the music theater this next year. There are five shows!"

"Did you find anything?" Charles asked her.

Elizabeth looked over towards the table. "Five laptops. They would be a great start for the computer lab I would like to begin."

"Well, I hope you get them," Charles said.

"Me, too." She shrugged as she looked back at him. "I doubt I bid high enough, though." She glanced back at the computers. "Maybe I should go back and raise my bid."

"Many people do go back during the course of the evening and raise their bids." Charles laughed. "Even though they may already have the highest bid!" He leaned in. "A little word of advice. If you see a lot of people hanging around the item, chances are the bids will be high. Just peek in occasionally, to see if anyone else is eyeing it."

"Thanks, and I hope you win the bid for the theater!" She

looked down at the tickets. "Oh, I see Will donated these, too."

"Yes, he donates quite a few items. He purchases four season passes every year and always auctions off two of them."

Elizabeth laughed. "I certainly hope he enjoys the company of whoever wins the bid!"

"Well, hopefully it will be me!" Charles said with a laugh.

They finished walking around the room together, and then stepped out into the long hallway.

Charles looked down at his watch and said, "I imagine the dancing will begin soon. Why don't we head for the ballroom?"

"You two go on ahead. I think I will go check out the library."

"Are you certain, Lizzy? You don't have to do this."

"Do what?"

"Leave so Charles and I can be alone."

Elizabeth smiled. "You do enjoy being alone with Charles, don't you?"

When Jane meekly nodded, Elizabeth said, "And I will be perfectly content looking through that library." She gave a shrug. "I will join you shortly."

Elizabeth quickly turned before Jane had a chance to object.

She made her way down the long hall to the library, stepped in, and looked about her. It was beautiful, with tall mahogany bookcases, and even a rolling ladder to get up to the top shelves. Garlands of holly were wrapped with red ribbon and bows draped across the top of the shelves, twinkling lights and candles glistened on a small table, a small, decorated Christmas tree stood in the far corner, and several nativities were set up in different places around the room – on shelves, on tables, and on the main desk.

She walked over to a beautiful marble nativity and ran her fingers lightly over the smooth, cool figures.

She moved to the bookshelves and glanced at the titles and authors of the books, some of which were quite old. They also seemed to be in order by topic and author, with the topics listed at the top of the shelf.

"Very well organized," she said softly. "And I wouldn't be surprised if there were several first editions."

"Unfortunately, there are no first editions, but several second and third."

Elizabeth quickly turned, surprised to see that Will had walked in. She drew in a silent breath.

"Oh, I hope you do not mind me coming in to snoop a little bit. I noticed it when we walked past earlier. I don't think there is anything finer than a well-stocked library."

Will gave a shrug. "I agree, as long as it is a well-read library, as well. A well-stocked library that is not well-read is… well, useless." He smiled, revealing his elusive dimple.

Elizabeth gave a nod in agreement. "I am astonished with the meticulous order of all the books. It appears someone cares greatly about it." She lifted her brow in his direction.

"Some of these books have been in the family for almost a hundred years. I would hope they're greatly cared for."

Will smiled and leaned against a bookshelf, crossing his arms. "Have you enjoyed yourself so far?"

"Oh, yes! Charles has been the most delightful host and has introduced us to several people."

Will smiled. "I am glad." He gave a nod of his head towards the ceiling. "But you really ought to be careful where you stand in this house at Christmas. My grandmother has a penchant for…"

Elizabeth glanced up. "Mistletoe!" She stepped back quickly. "Don't even think of trying to kiss me, Will Darcy, or I might have to slap you!"

He gave a slight bow. "I would not be so brazen."

She chuckled nervously. "Your home is truly beautiful, and all the decorations are stunning."

He laughed. "My home? Heavens, no! This is my grandmother's home."

Elizabeth's eyes widened. "Oh, I beg your pardon, but Charles told Jane the Christmas Gala was at your house."

He smiled. "We have been friends for a long time, having met at a summer camp when we were about eight years old. I lived here with my family, and Charles probably said he was going over to Will's house when invited over, as any child would say. Despite not living here anymore, I guess old habits are hard to lose."

"I see."

"I have a townhouse close to my office." He gave a shrug. "However, I do have a room here in the house that is mine to use whenever I need it. Like tonight, for example, as it will likely be a late night."

"Would that room, perchance, be the room where the auction is being held – and your bed located under one of the tables?" She lifted her brows and tilted her head.

Will wagged his finger at her. "I would wager that you have been talking to my grandmother. She loves to tell that story."

"Well, everything is beautiful. I love all the nativities in this room." She looked towards the desk. "Especially the marble one."

"My grandmother has set up this room so that it only contains decorations pertinent to the first Christmas. If you look closely, the tree is decorated with stars, angels, sheep, and of course, miniatures of Joseph, Mary, and the baby Jesus."

Elizabeth pointed towards the ceiling. "And the mistletoe?"

Will shrugged. "My grandmother has a mischievous streak in her, but I'm certain they had mistletoe back then."

Elizabeth smiled and opened her mouth to say something but stopped when that same shrill voice she heard earlier broke the silence.

"Will! There you are! Your grandmother is looking for you! They are about…" Caroline Bingley stepped in further and noticed Elizabeth. She drew back, her eyes darkening. "It's about time… for the first dance!"

"Please tell her I will be there shortly."

Caroline frowned, muttered an agreement, and left.

"For several years, my grandmother and I have had the tradition of dancing the first dance together, so if you will excuse me…"

"Of course! I wouldn't wish to spoil any traditions!"

Will began to walk away but stopped and looked back. "Do you know how to waltz?"

Elizabeth laughed. "I do. My mother didn't make Jane and me take dance lessons for nothing!"

Will smiled. "Would you dance the second with me? We always dance to *The Christmas Waltz*."

Elizabeth could barely fathom an answer, and was only able to murmur, "Of course."

When he stepped out, Elizabeth found herself grasping the shelf of one of the bookcases for support, reprimanding herself for having agreed to dance with him.

Chapter 7

Elizabeth lingered in the library attempting to figure out what just happened… and why. She wondered if he was making amends for his declaration at the restaurant that he did not wish to dance with her. She shook her head recollecting that she'd been the first to say she wasn't inclined to dance with him.

She drew in a breath, steeled herself, and set out towards the ballroom. She heard someone begin talking about the traditional first dance and how it used to be danced by Evelyn Darcy and her husband, then when he died, with her son, and now the tradition continued with her grandson, Will.

She found Jane and Charles and walked up to their side.

Jane grasped her arm. "Isn't this sweet? They have danced the first dance together since his father died."

"Yes," Elizabeth said as she watched the tender scene unfold before her. It was apparent that his grandmother was very fond of Will, as she looked up at him with a wide smile and twinkling eyes. They were barely moving on the dance floor, but they both seemed to be enjoying it.

"Lizzy, are you all right? You look rather pale."

Elizabeth touched her fingers to her cheek. "I do?" She gave a shrug. "Perhaps I am just tired." She looked about her at everyone who had gathered around the room watching the pair dance. "Do you suppose the next song will be open to everyone?"

Jane gave a shrug. "I suppose we'll soon find out."

Elizabeth gulped. "That, we will."

"Why do you ask?"

Elizabeth shook her head. "You will see."

When the dance ended, the elderly lady reached up on her toes and kissed her grandson.

"You can see she adores him!" Jane said.

Elizabeth nodded mutely.

When the dance ended, it was announced that the next dance would be the traditional waltz to *The Christmas Waltz*.

Elizabeth watched as Will walked over to her. He extended his hand, and when she took it, she heard Jane gasp.

As they began to walk to the center of the dance floor, she was suddenly aware of all the eyes upon them. Her hand felt warm in his, and yet she felt a shiver course through her. They came to the center of the floor, and the carolers who had been outside began to gather by the microphones.

When other couples walked out onto the floor, she relaxed. Will seemed to notice.

"Were you a little apprehensive thinking we would be the only ones on the dance floor?"

Elizabeth let out a nervous chuckle. "No, not just a little. I was *very* apprehensive that we would be the only ones on the dance floor. Hopefully now if I misstep, no one will notice."

"I am certain they will not."

"I enjoyed watching you and your grandmother. It is apparent you both really care for each other."

"Well, I can speak for myself that I do greatly care for her. She is a special lady."

"I can see that."

"She used to begin the dance with this waltz. Now she has difficulty walking, and the waltz is out of the question. She still wants to open the dancing, but insists the waltz be reserved for those who have the ability to do so."

The emcee announced the song. "Ladies and gentlemen, please enjoy this rendition of *The Christmas Waltz* sung by the Holiday Harmonizer carolers."

Will turned and placed his hand around Elizabeth just below her shoulder. He took her hand in his other hand, while she reached up and placed her hand on his shoulder.

Just as the song was about to begin, Will said, "There is nothing to worry about, but there is one thing I should probably tell you in advance."

Elizabeth gave him a questioning look. "And what's that?"

"It's been a tradition that we do a dip at the end of the waltz. Have you ever been dipped?"

Elizabeth let out a breath. "I've seen others do it, but I have never done it myself."

"When the music slows at the end of the song, I'll ease you down to your left. Just relax and trust that I'll support you and not let you fall."

Elizabeth laughed nervously. "Can I trust you not to drop me?"

"Don't worry. I'll let you know when it's about to happen."

The music started, and the carolers began singing, "Frosted window panes…"

Elizabeth enjoyed how easy it was to follow him. She felt light on her feet, and they danced in synchronized moves to the music. He was a much better partner than her father and Jane, whom she often practiced with, as well as the young, awkward boys who were her partners in dance class.

She also loved Will's cologne. Ardently. It was the one she had smelled at the store, and now she struggled to keep herself from drawing nearer to him just to take a better whiff.

She was lost in a whirl of thoughts, movement, and reverie when Will looked down. "The song is about to end. Are you ready?"

Elizabeth looked up with a questioning glance. "Ready?"

"The dip."

Her eyes widened. "Do I have any other option?"

Instead of answering, he began to bend down towards her as his arm at her back gently lowered her. She lifted her hand from his shoulder and extended it out, as she had seen done before.

He didn't bring her up immediately, and they gazed at each other for a moment. Elizabeth felt she could barely breathe.

The moment ended, and Will slowly brought her back up. Elizabeth readily noticed many eyes upon them.

She smiled nervously. "Thank you. I enjoyed it."

"As did I."

He escorted her to the side of the room where Charles and Jane stood.

"I saw you out there dancing, Charles," Will said. You have improved. I didn't think you would ever waltz again after last year's attempt."

He let out a laugh. "Jane convinced me I could do it. She is a great leader!"

Will let out a muffled laugh.

Charles smiled. "I was pleasantly surprised to see you on the dance floor with Elizabeth. You normally dance with Georgiana."

Elizabeth turned and looked at Will in surprise. With a nod of his head towards the other side of the room, he said, "As you can see, Georgie has another gentleman in her life, and she begged off the waltz with me to dance with him."

"Oh!" his friend exclaimed. "I hadn't even noticed them." He smiled at Jane. "Jane is the only person I had my eyes on."

Jane blushed slightly, and Will only shook his head.

Elizabeth was glad for the conversation between the two men, as it allowed her to examine both the man with whom she had just danced and her feelings towards him. She couldn't think straight around him and finally decided she should leave.

"If you don't mind, I think I will be heading home now." She turned to Will. "Thank you, Will, for a lovely evening. I truly enjoyed myself."

"Are you sure you have to leave?" Jane asked.

"I think I must. You all enjoy the rest of the evening. I will see myself out."

"Please, wait," Will said. "I'd be delighted to escort you out."

Elizabeth was about to tell him that was unnecessary, but instead, said, "Thank you."

Before leaving, she walked over to his grandmother and expressed her delight in watching her and Will dance.

"Oh, pshaw! That wasn't dancing. He was merely holding me up so I wouldn't fall!" She laughed and winked at her grandson. "But I thank you for your kind sentiment." She tilted her head. "I hope I see you here again. It's been a pleasure meeting you."

"Thank you, but the pleasure has been all mine."

She and Will walked to the small check room where she retrieved her coat and purse, and Will helped her put her coat on. Then they stepped outside.

"Ooh, it is cold!" Elizabeth said. "I think it might start snowing soon."

"I believe you may be right," he replied. "My grandmother had hoped the freezing weather would hold off until after the Gala so she could keep the pond filled with water. Now that the Gala is over, she will have it emptied."

"It truly adds a Christmas magic to the home, reflecting all the lights."

The valet came up and took her claim ticket from her, telling her he would return with her car in a few minutes.

After a few moments of silence, Will looked at Elizabeth and said, "I hope you didn't feel as though you were put on the spot earlier."

Elizabeth looked up. "You mean when you asked me to dance the waltz with you?" When he nodded, she said, "Well, you did at least ask me ahead of time if I could waltz. And I did enjoy it." She could have also added how light on her feet he made her feel, how secure, how heavenly his cologne was, how handsome…

"I am glad. I came upon you just after my sister informed me that she was going to waltz with her boyfriend. I wasn't sure what I was going to do about the dance."

"I see." A surprising wave of disappointment flooded her, and she gave her head a shake to rid herself of it. "Oh, here is my car," she said, grateful she would now be able to leave.

"Did you purchase a new car since I saw you last?"

She looked at him and then the car. "Oh, no," she said with a laugh. "It's my father's car. He loaned it to us tonight because he thought…" She paused for a moment. "He thought we would be more comfortable in it as we were wearing long gowns and all."

"You… and your sister looked very nice tonight."

Breathe, she told herself. "Thank you. And thank you again for a lovely evening. I truly enjoyed it."

"I am glad," he replied. "Good night, Elizabeth."

Elizabeth wished him a good night as she walked to the car. The valet stepped out of the car and held the door open for her as she walked towards him.

She wanted to look back at Will, but she was certain he would be gone. He had made it perfectly clear to her that dancing with her had happened solely because she had been at the right place at the right time. He probably offered to walk her out to give him the opportunity to make that clear. It was nothing more.

She smiled at the valet and thanked him, telling herself not to turn back to see if Will was still there. Just as she was about to step in the car, she felt a single snowflake fall on her nose. She glanced up and saw that snowflakes were beginning to fall.

Without thinking, she turned back to where Will had been

standing and saw that he was still there. She took in a quick breath of surprise. "It is beginning to snow!"

"I believe you're right," he said. "Drive safely."

"Thank you. I will."

"And Merry Christmas, Elizabeth."

"Same to you," she replied and stepped into the car.

She gripped the steering wheel and peered up into her rear-view mirror to see he had still not moved. She let out a huff, saying, "Will Darcy, you are making it exceedingly difficult to prove Jane wrong regarding my feelings for you! Exceedingly difficult!"

Chapter 8

Will watched Elizabeth pull away in her car - her father's car - until she was no longer in sight.

He glanced up to the sky and felt a few snowflakes land on his face, prompting him to smile. Snow didn't always make him smile, but he felt like smiling now. He felt like smiling about all the decorations his grandmother had put up for the Gala each year, the Christmas songs that had begun playing several weeks ago, and he even smiled knowing the crowds of people he would be encountering once he stepped back inside.

He realized he was whistling as he walked through the front door. "What is it about her that fills me with such joy?" he whispered with a breathy laugh.

His smile quickly disappeared when Caroline Bingley marched up to him. "Where have you been? We've been looking for you."

"We?" Will asked. "Who is we?"

Caroline drew in a long breath. "Well, I have, and I know Charles wondered where you went." She gave a nod toward the auction room. "They'll be announcing the winning bids soon." Tilting her head, she said, "I'm sure you'll want to know who you will be sitting with at the five theater performances. I understand the musicals this season are some of the best."

Will ignored her hint and looked down at his watch. "The bidding closes in fifteen minutes. I am going to see if there is anything I want to bid on." He looked back up at her. "Please excuse me."

"Oh, certainly." She turned towards the ballroom. "I believe there are still a few dances left." She lifted a brow as she sent him a hopeful glance.

"I suppose you're right." Will turned and walked into the room.

There were a few people making some last-minute bids, and Will greeted them. He really wasn't interested in anything save for the computers he knew Elizabeth had bid on. When he walked up, he peeked in the basket containing the bids, noticing quite a few. He rubbed his chin as he contemplated that Elizabeth would likely not have bid high enough to win. He drew in a breath and picked up one of the printed bid sheets and quickly filled it out. He then dropped it in the box.

His heart soared, while still not completely understanding why. As he walked to the ballroom, knowing he would encounter Caroline and several others who were solely focused on material things, he thought about this unexpected attraction to Elizabeth.

He reasoned that she was obviously intelligent, had a caring and giving heart, seemed not at all interested in money or the trappings of wealth, and she was fun and lively. His shoulders rose as he drew in a breath and then lowered as he slowly let it out.

His musings were interrupted by a couple whose names he couldn't recall, but he knew they were acquaintances of his aunt and uncle. They thanked him for the lovely evening.

"It has just begun to snow, so please take care driving home. And thank you for coming... Mr. and Mrs. Holcomb."

They walked away, and he smiled that he finally remembered their name.

His ability to recollect names was still strong, although perhaps somewhat slower at present due to his unexpected preoccupation with one Elizabeth Bennet.

He stepped into the ballroom and began swaying to the song that was being played. He felt a light hand on his shoulder, and thinking it was Caroline again, he quickly spun around.

Instead of Caroline, it was his grandmother. He breathed a sigh of relief and smiled. "Hello, Grandmother. You have outdone yourself again."

"Pshaw!" she replied with a wave of her hand. "I do nothing, only give the orders."

Will chuckled.

His grandmother looked about. "You seem much more at ease than you normally do. In fact, you seem almost... jovial."

"Jovial?"

"Could this perhaps have something to do with that sweet young lady you danced with earlier?"

Will dropped his head and looked at his shoes, as if he were a little boy suddenly rendered shy.

His grandmother cleared her throat. "I noticed you disappeared soon after the dance."

He looked up and met her questioning glance. "She had to leave. I walked her out."

"Did you?" The lines around her eyes deepened as she smiled. "Good for you." She leaned in conspiratorially. "I like her."

"Really?" He tilted his head. "And what do you like about her?"

She reached out her frail hand and grasped his. "She seems kind, friendly, and authentic."

"Authentic?"

"Yes, that is it. She does not seem impressed with money and who's who, and that kind of thing. Authentic."

Will smiled. "I believe you are right."

She patted his hand and then gave it a squeeze. "Mind you, don't let her get away."

Will chuckled. "We aren't even..."

She wagged her finger. "I know, my dear. Just don't let her get away."

He leaned over and gave his grandmother a kiss. "I always appreciate your wise advice."

They both turned toward the couples on the dance floor as Caroline walked over to them. His grandmother let out a soft huff and turned to walk away.

Caroline came and stood beside him, letting out a long sigh. "Oh, I just love this song. It reminds me so much of Christmas - the snow, the decorations, especially when dancing to it."

Will briefly closed his eyes. "It is "Away in a Manger," and I don't believe they had snow or decorations on that first Christmas." He gripped his hand into a fist. "And I'm certain there was no dancing in the manger."

Caroline was not dissuaded, and her eyes lit up. "But perhaps they did dance. I'm certain they felt like dancing."

Will stifled a groan, but he was in too good a mood to let Caroline's nonsense bother him.

"Would you care to dance?" He knew the song was almost finished and figured he could handle a short dance with her.

"Oh! I would love to!"

He escorted her to the floor, and they began to dance. He

attempted to hold her at arm's length, but she was persistent in drawing much closer than he would have preferred.

As they danced, he thought about the differences between Caroline and Elizabeth. He trusted his grandmother's insight and agreed with her assessment. Elizabeth was, as his grandmother had said, "kind, friendly, and authentic." He thought back to their first meeting. She had not been overtly kind or friendly, but she had certainly been authentic.

Caroline, on the other hand, was devious, conniving, and duplicitous. How she and Charles could be siblings, he had no idea. They were...

"What can we do about Charles and Jane?"

Will shook his head. "What about Charles and Jane?"

"Certainly, you must realize how unsuited they are for each other." Caroline turned her head towards the couple, who were dancing particularly close to one another. "Charles deserves so much better. Her family lives in the northeast side of town. And her sister works in one of the poorest neighborhoods around. The children she must deal with!"

The song came to an end, and Caroline let out a moan. "Oh, that wasn't long enough."

"I am sorry, Caroline, but I must see to my grandmother. If you will excuse me." He walked away, and while his spirits were still soaring because of Elizabeth, they had been brought down a little because of Caroline. Just a little.

Chapter 9

The next morning, Elizabeth awoke when the first rays of the sun peeked through the curtains in her room. In the moment that her eyes opened, her thoughts went to the Christmas Gala the night before… the home, the decorations, and… Will Darcy. Images of their meeting in the library, the waltz, and his watching her as she got into her car and drove away persisted.

She ran her fingers through her hair, smoothing out some tangles. She let out a small cry as she encountered some stubborn ones that pulled too hard. Pounding her hands down onto the bed, she pushed herself up. She was determined to put thoughts of that man out of her mind.

She had allowed herself to indulge in the festive Christmas atmosphere at the Gala. While enjoying the beautiful decorations, excellent music, delightful food, and especially dancing the waltz with him, she had given little thought to the children in PREP and the meager Christmas most would have. At least they would have a nice Christmas party.

She let out a sigh as she thought about how much she had enjoyed talking to some of the people there about her work. While a few merely gave her a condescending smile, there were others who truly seemed interested in what she was doing.

Climbing out of bed, she put on her robe, walking slowly to the window to look out. A light dusting of snow rested on the grass, bushes, and branches of the trees, glistening in the sunlight. Fortunately, the streets were clear. She was glad for that.

She heard movement in Jane's room and smiled. She was eager to hear how Jane had enjoyed the evening. She stepped out of her room and tapped on her door. Jane bade her enter.

Elizabeth peeked in. "Well?" she asked in a long drawl and with eyebrows lifted in anticipation.

Jane let out a long sigh. "I had a most delightful time with

Charles. He is so…" She lifted her shoulders and let out another sigh. She looked at Elizabeth and smiled. "Perfect," she said in a whisper.

Elizabeth came to her side and wrapped her in a hug. "I'm so happy for you. I do like him!"

"He is coming by this afternoon, and we are going to a movie and then dinner."

"Going out with him two nights in a row? I fear, Jane, that soon I may never see you! But I am delighted!"

"Oh, and he won the auction bid for the season tickets to the music theater."

Elizabeth laughed. "It is a good thing Will and Charles are such good friends, as the two will be seated beside each other for five performances."

Elizabeth sat down on Jane's bed as her sister looked through her closet for the clothes she would wear. She pulled out a sweater and a pair of pants. "What do you think about these?" Jane held them up.

"Jane, it's silly that you feel you have to ask me what you ought to wear. You are the style expert, and in addition, everything you wear looks good on you as you are so beautiful."

"Oh, Lizzy, you exaggerate."

Elizabeth gave a shrug. "You, my dear sister, are too modest."

There was silence for a moment, and then Elizabeth asked, "Do you, by any chance, know who won the computers in the auction?"

Jane turned quickly. "Oh, no, we didn't stay to hear all the winners. I am certain they'll notify you if you won."

"I suppose, but I'm not holding my breath."

"Do you have any plans today?"

"I have to return Dad's car, and then I am going to PREP to do a little work for the Christmas party. Since you and Charles will be eating out, I'll have the leftover taco soup we served the kids the other day."

"There is nothing better than your taco soup."

"Especially when I can add some spices and peppers to it, now that the children won't be eating it." She laughed. "I'll probably also see what decorations I have from previous Christmas parties to make things look a little more festive." She let out a sigh. "I guess I'd better get busy, as the party is next week."

"I hope you'll be pleased with the new company helping with it."

Elizabeth looked down at her hands. "I hope so, too, but whatever they do will be better than nothing."

~~*

After showering, getting dressed, and enjoying a quick breakfast, Elizabeth exchanged cars with her dad and then set off for PREP. As she was pulling into the small parking lot, her phone rang. She glanced at it, and with no name coming up and not recognizing the number, she didn't answer it. She knew if it was important, they would leave a message.

Elizabeth unlocked the door and stepped in; the cold air of the building enveloping her, and she pulled her coat tightly about her. She walked over to the thermostat and turned it up so the heater would come on. She had been trying to conserve both electricity and funds, and with the cold that had come through last night, it was quite chilly. She decided to keep her coat on until the heat warmed everything up.

She went into the small kitchen and pulled out the crockpot from one of the cupboards. She dumped the container of leftover taco soup into it and turned it on, adding some jalapeños and chipotle peppers to it, as well as some additional spices.

She heard the ping of a phone message being left and pulled out her phone. She pressed voicemail and listened as a female's voice began speaking.

"Hello, Elizabeth, this is Georgiana Darcy. I would like to let you know that you won the computers in last night's auction..."

Elizabeth's jaw dropped, and she shook her head as she brought her attention back to the conversation. "If you would please call me back, we can arrange for their delivery. Let me know if today would be convenient. And thank you for participating in the auction."

She could barely breathe as she considered what a blessing this was! Having the computers would be wonderful for the children, and her mind began swirling with thoughts of setting up a computer lab.

She called Georgiana back, but receiving no answer, she left a voicemail herself. She told Georgiana that she would be at her PREP facility for the remainder of the day and gave her the address in Meryton Heights. She concluded by telling her that they could park on the side of the building and to come to the front door and ring the bell so she could let them in.

With that done, she began cleaning, and when she was finished, the room had warmed up enough that she could take off her coat. As she walked past her phone, she heard the ping of another voicemail. She gave her head a frustrated shake as she realized she missed another call and picked up her phone to listen.

"Hello, this is Georgiana, again. It seems we are playing phone tag. I can send someone over right away. Again congratulations."

Elizabeth looked around the room as she tried to determine where the best place for the computers would be. There was a side wall where she could place two rectangular tables which would be long enough to hold the computers. She walked over and slid several cube storage units closer to each other to make room for the tables. Then she pushed a floor lamp in the opposite direction.

She stood back and looked at the now open space and gave a nod of approval. An electrical outlet was directly behind it, so getting everything hooked up should be easy enough.

A wide smile lit her face. "There! That should be perfect!" She was able to easily slide the two tables into the spot.

She turned on some Christmas music and then went to a back storeroom and was lost in going through holiday decorations when the doorbell rang. "Oh!" she said as she clapped her hands. "My computers must be here!"

She rushed to the door and opened it, neglecting to even peek through the peep hole to see who it was. She did a double take when she saw Will Darcy standing there. She opened her mouth to speak, but nothing came forth.

"Hello, Elizabeth. May I come in?"

"Oh! Of course! I'm sorry!" She opened the door and took in a deep breath as he walked past carrying several boxes.

"Where would you like the computers?"

When Elizabeth did not answer, he turned back to her and sent her a questioning glance.

"Over here, please" she pointed to the tables.

He walked over and put the boxes down.

"I need to make a couple more trips out to the car to bring them all in."

"All right. You can keep the door unlocked while you are doing that."

He made two trips out to his car, came back in, and took off his long black, wool coat, placing it over a chair. Elizabeth's next surprise was that he was wearing jeans and a casual sweater. She was not used to seeing him in such informal attire, and she was surprised at how attractive she found him to be.

"I think you will be pleased with these computers. They come with several applications."

"I still can't believe I won the bid. I didn't really bid that much higher than the minimum bid."

Will cast a sideways glance at her and gave a shrug. "You never know with the sealed bid auctions. You don't know how many people are bidding on the items, let alone the amount they bid."

"That's true. I'm delighted, but still surprised."

"A nice surprise, I hope?"

"Oh, definitely. "

Elizabeth watched him for a while and then said, "If you don't mind, I'll be in my office if you need anything. It's just in the back."

"Sure," he replied as he pulled out the cables from the box.

Elizabeth sat down at her computer, glancing over at Will occasionally. She could see him through the open door, and he worked effortlessly and quickly. He didn't seem like the same man from the restaurant or the Christmas Gala, and that made it more difficult to maintain her opinion of him.

She had to chuckle when she heard him humming along to the Christmas music she had put on.

"How many different sides to you are there?" she whispered softly. If he started singing, she wouldn't know what to think.

As it neared noon, her stomach began growling, and she could smell the taco soup that was heating in the crockpot.

She walked out of her office and saw that Will was sitting at one of the computers.

"I don't know how much longer you'll be working, but I have some leftover taco soup heating if you'd like some lunch. I'm going to have some now."

He quickly turned around, and a smile touched his lips, producing his small dimple. "I'm just about done. Taco soup sounds great. I've been smelling it, and it smells terrific."

"It isn't much. It's just leftovers."

"Well, I understand that soup always tastes better the next day."

Elizabeth smiled. "So, they say. I'll get it ready."

She walked into the kitchen and pulled out two soup bowls and spoons, a couple of napkins, and a bag of tortilla chips. As she was ladling the soup into the bowls, she noticed out of the corner of her eye that Will stood at the doorway. He leaned against the door jamb, and his arms were crossed at his chest.

"I've finished installing the computers. Is there something I can do to help with lunch?"

She couldn't think straight, and she finally answered, "Could you get two glasses out of that cupboard and put some ice in them? I have iced tea in the refrigerator, we have water, and I think there is a little lemonade left." She paused and looked up at him. "Unless you want coffee... or hot chocolate."

"No, iced tea is fine."

"I'll have iced tea also. There is sugar in the little bowl if you want it sweetened."

Will shook his head. "I drink it plain. You?"

"I drink it plain, as well."

Will poured the drinks, and Elizabeth told him to put them on the small table in the kitchen. That was where she normally ate when she was by herself.

Elizabeth brought the bowls, chips, and napkins over, and then opened the refrigerator and took out some shredded cheese.

"You can sprinkle some of this on top, along with the tortilla chips if you like."

"Thanks. I think I will."

When they both sat down, Elizabeth quickly regretted the decision to sit at the small table with him. It seemed a little too intimate for her.

Will took a few bites of the soup and then held out his spoon. "Whoa! This is really good! Hot, but good!"

"Oh, I'm sorry. I should have asked if you like your food spicy. I make it mild for the children, but I added some peppers for me."

Will looked down at his spoon and then back to Elizabeth. "I do like things spicy. The spicier the better." He smiled and then put the spoon in his mouth.

Elizabeth felt her cheeks warm a bit and turned her attention back to her own bowl of soup.

They ate in silence for a short while, and at length, Will asked, "So what sets PREP apart from other day… tutoring centers?"

Elizabeth bit her lip and looked him squarely in the eye. "It isn't just a tutoring center. We focus on the differences in learning styles. We work with each child to see how they best learn, how they can become more motivated to learn, and we are able to work with them when there is a real impediment."

"I see. Like ADHD?"

Elizabeth slowly nodded. "In college, my studies had an emphasis on different learning styles."

"Special needs education?'

"Not quite." She took a sip of the soup. "Special needs education often focuses on those with fairly severe handicaps of all kinds. I wanted to focus on the neurotypical child who has trouble learning and find out why."

Will leaned in. "Is there a reason you wanted to pursue this specific field?"

Elizabeth looked down and began swirling her spoon around in the bowl. She glanced back up and said very slowly, "I was one of those students."

Will's brows lifted. "Indeed?"

She slowly brought her spoon up to her lips. "I had trouble reading when I was younger. I really struggled when I had to read something out loud."

"Dyslexia?"

"Actually, no. It turned out to be something that wasn't a severe hindrance. With the help of my second-grade teacher and encouragement to get tested, it was determined I have a small blind spot in the very center of my right eye. When I tried to read – and it mainly happened when I was reading aloud – the words would disappear and jump around."

"And what did this teacher do to help you?"

"She encouraged my parents to have an eye examination, and then showed me exercises to do that helped my other eye become the dominant eye."

"You don't have any trouble with it anymore?"

Elizabeth chuckled. "Well, I do struggle on eye tests when they are testing just the right eye. When the letters get too small, there is literally a small black blur over the letter. To help me see the letter, I have to look a little to the left or right of that blur."

"Sounds like something you can live with."

"Yes, and I have since learned that I would have eventually compensated for it on my own, but it was very distressing to me when everything else came so easy to me. That distress is what I remember most, and what I want to help children avoid, if I can."

"That is very interesting." Will began tapping his fingers on the table.

"The whole ordeal of struggling to read aloud, having the other children laugh at me and make fun of me and not knowing why, had begun to erode my self-esteem." She shook her head slowly and looked down into her bowl of soup. She glanced back up. "That is why I chose tutoring with a focus on learning differences and difficulties."

"I see. Another question if you don't mind."

"Sure."

"Why Meryton Heights?"

Elizabeth's breath hitched as she felt her insides tighten with indignation. She let her breath out slowly and asked, "Why not?"

Will's eyes narrowed. "Elizabeth Bennet, I'm certain you are capable of being more articulate in your answer than that."

Elizabeth glanced down at her hands, which were now tight fists in her lap. She slowly looked up. "As a student teacher, I taught in a public school here. One of the students, Melissa Morell, had difficulty learning. The school didn't have the funds to do special testing, so I began to work with her, figuring out a way to help her learn. She really struggled with math."

"Were you able to help her?"

Elizabeth looked down and blinked away tears that had begun to fill her eyes. "Yes, I did it by teaching her music. Melissa was a natural, and she enjoyed learning to play the piano so much that she didn't even realize at first that she was learning math concepts that are intrinsic to music theory."

"And how is she doing now?"

It was a moment before Elizabeth answered. When she looked

up, Will was leaning in. "Did something happen?" he asked.

Elizabeth bit her bottom lip briefly, and replied softly, "Yes. She was... she was killed in a car accident a few years later."

Will drew back. "I am so sorry. What happened?"

Elizabeth made a futile attempt to hold back both the tears that threatened to spill and the anger that was about to boil over. She stood up and reached for a tissue. "There was another driver... he ran a red light as Mrs. Morell, her mother, was turning. The car..." Her hands began to shake, and she brought one hand up to wipe away a tear. "The car hit her car on the back passenger side where Melissa was sitting."

"I am sorry."

"She was in the hospital for a week before her little body gave up fighting." Elizabeth turned away as she wiped her eyes. "Her younger sister is now in our program."

"And the other driver?"

Elizabeth closed her eyes and fisted her hands again. "He was... he was from a..." She drew in a ragged breath. "He basically got off with a slap on the wrist. When Mrs. Morell brought a civil suit against him to help her pay for the hospital bills and the time off she had to take while Melissa was in the hospital, his lawyer turned things around and ended up making Mrs. Morell feel as though it was all her fault." She dropped her hands to her side. "To this day, she feels a great sense of guilt that she shouldn't feel!"

Elizabeth turned to pick up her half-empty bowl and put it on the counter by the sink, no longer hungry. "Let's speak of something else."

Will was quiet, and when Elizabeth sat down at the table again, she tried to smile. "Jane tells me Charles won the bid for the musical theater tickets."

"He did."

"You must be glad you will be sitting with someone you know and whose company you enjoy."

Will gave a shrug. "I knew most people at the Gala, so it would have been fine with anyone who won."

"I hear the first performance is a musical written by a local woman."

"Yes. I understand it's very good. I believe it's called *Hindsight,* and the writer hopes to eventually get it performed on

Broadway.”

“That would be very exciting.”

Will looked down at his soup, giving it a stir, and then looked back up. “Would you want to… to go with me to see it?”

Elizabeth’s eyes shot up and met his. “With you?”

Will nodded.

She waved her hands in the air. “I hope you don’t think that I brought up the subject hoping you would invite me.”

“Not at all.”

Elizabeth dropped her head. “I don’t know. I’m not sure...”

“Look. It doesn’t have to be a date.” He gave a shrug and leaned back into his chair, but he kept his eyes on her. “It will just be you and Jane and Charles and me.”

Elizabeth’s brows furrowed. “Let me think about it.”

“Sure,” Will said. “You have time to decide. The season begins in February.”

He stood up and pulled out his business card, placing it on the table. “If you have any issues with any of the computers, feel free to give me a call.” He pointed to the card. “This is my personal phone number.

She stood up. “Thank you. I’m sure everything will be fine.” She blew out a puff of air. “If you don’t mind, I am going to disappear in the back storage room. I am trying to find things for our Christmas party.”

“You’re able to have a party, then? I remember you mentioned at the restaurant that you didn’t think you were going to be able to have one.”

“Yes, another company – F&D, I believe – became aware that Mr. Forster was no longer able to do it and offered to help.”

“I’m glad to hear that.” He paused and then asked, “Is there anything I can do for the party?”

Elizabeth looked up quickly. “Thank you, but no. You’ve done so much already. I appreciate your offer, but we’ll manage fine.”

“Are you certain?”

Elizabeth drew in a breath. “I wouldn’t wish to be...” She shook her head. “Yes, I am certain.”

Chapter 10

On the day of PREP's Christmas party, Elizabeth looked about her at all the decorations that adorned the room. The cookies and cupcakes she and the other tutors had made were placed on serving platters, large drink dispensers were filled with water and fruit punch, and they were now just waiting for the first children to arrive.

She felt a surge of joy and gratefulness that she had finally begun to feel the stirrings of that elusive Christmas spirit that had been missing since Mr. Forster had called. But after receiving the call from F&D, it had given her the incentive she needed to put up the rest of the holiday decorations. Attending the Christmas Gala had certainly helped, as well. She then thought of Will, and shook her head, willing all thoughts of him to be gone.

As she sat in the large room waiting, she glanced at the tree adorned with twinkling lights and handmade ornaments that had been made throughout the month. The students would be taking all the ornaments home today, as well as the ones they would make at the party. She had Christmas music softly playing and some pine scented oils diffusing into the air. She inhaled the scent and smiled. Yes, it felt good to have her Christmas spirit back.

Almost. There was still the uncertainty of the future of PREP, with the inevitable closing of these doors, due to the new convention center being built.

"Kamie, have I forgotten anything?"

Kamie stepped out from the kitchen. "I think you've gone above and beyond what needs to be done. Everything looks, sounds, and smells great!" She let out a laugh. "I can't wait to taste all these goodies!"

The buzzer rang, and Elizabeth lifted her hands. "That must be Laura with our little friends. And so, it begins!"

Elizabeth opened the door, and the children burst through,

aware that today was going to be different. Instead of quietly working together in groups on their homework and tutoring, and playing games that helped them learn, they would be playing Christmas games, having delicious treats, singing carols, and at the end of the day, there would be a special treat for them.

When all the students had arrived, Elizabeth, Laura, and Kamie began rotating smaller groups through the crafts, games, and telling them the Christmas story.

Elizabeth allowed for their overabundant display of excitement, as this was, after all, a Christmas party. There were only a few of them who needed to be reminded that despite being a party, they still needed to act politely and kindly. For the most part, however, they did well, and after finishing the group activities, they enjoyed singing some familiar Christmas carols.

The time passed quickly, and when the buzzer rang at four-thirty, Elizabeth looked at Laura. "Would you go see who that is, please?" She gave her a wink and a smile, knowing that their Santa, someone named Richard, had arrived right on time.

After a few moments, Laura came to the door and clasped her hands in front of her. "Boys and girls, we have a special guest who has joined us this afternoon. It is someone who always brings a smile to your face, whether you are young or old."

A few of them yelled out, "Santa Claus!" which incited loud cheers of joy.

Laura stepped into the room followed by a man bellowing out in a deep voice, "Ho, ho, ho! Merry Christmas!" He was in a Santa outfit, with a wide girth, which Elizabeth surmised to be a pillow. He carried a large black sack, which he set down after inquiring where he was going to be seated.

She couldn't help but smile as she watched Santa walk around the room and cheerfully greet each child, asking their name. When he came up to Elizabeth, he held out his hand. "Hello, miss! Merry Christmas! And what is your name?"

"I am Elizabeth Bennet. I own Providence Readiness Excel Program, or PREP."

Santa wasn't particularly tall, and the only thing she could readily see were his eyes, which were bright blue and friendly. She didn't know if he was young or old, handsome or plain, but she liked Richard, whoever he was, and his portrayal of Santa.

"It is a pleasure to meet you, Miss Elizabeth Bennet. And have you been a good girl this year?"

Elizabeth laughed. "I hope I have been good enough!"

"Ho, ho, ho!" He looked at the students. "Did you hear that? Miss Bennet hopes she has been good enough. What do you think? Do you think she should get a present or a lump of coal?"

Half of them yelled out, "A present!" while a few others laughed and said, "A lump of coal!"

Elizabeth propped her hands on her hips. "Well, is that what some of you think of me?" She had the sternest look on her face, but then she began to laugh. "I guess I'll have to tell Santa about a few of your antics, then!"

Santa turned and whispered to Elizabeth. "How do you want to do this? I have to admit I've never been Santa before."

"Well, so far, you're doing great!"

"I thought I'd just pull out the gift and call the child's name to come up and sit on my lap, which would make it a little easier, since there are so many presents. They're all in gift bags and marked with their names."

"That sounds like an excellent idea. Now, some of the kids are older and might not want to sit on your lap. Don't be offended if they take their present and run."

"I won't be."

"I've told them, though, that they must be polite, so I will insist they thank you before they walk away." Elizabeth reached out and placed her hand on his shoulder. "And allow me to wholeheartedly thank you. I greatly appreciate this."

"It is my pleasure. Just let me know when you want to begin."

Beneath the fake Santa beard and mustache, Elizabeth could see that he smiled. "We can begin now. They are finishing up their ornaments and will come up when you call their name. After you hand out the presents, you'll be free to leave, as we will be eating our treats." She lifted a brow. "Unless you want to stay and join us?"

"Ho, ho, ho!" he laughed. "I saw those decorated sugar cookies when I walked in. I don't think I could pass them up!"

"You're more than welcome to stay and have some with us."

"Thanks." He paused and then added, "Do you mind if they wait to open their gifts until after I leave?"

"Certainly. We can at least try. Although, I can't guarantee that there won't be a few impatient ones who will struggle with just holding it in their hands." Elizabeth gave instructions to the children, that when their name was called, to go up to Santa and receive their gift, say thank you, and then bring it back to the table, where they would all open them together at the end.

She then stood back and let Richard be Santa. Despite never having played one, he did a great job, and she knew he'd likely be able to handle anything that came his way.

Elizabeth and her two tutors watched him in admiration as he interacted with the boys and girls. She felt a surge of Christmas delight as he appeared to take an interest in each child before handing them their gift bags. They seemed genuinely appreciative and each one remembered to thank him.

After the last child had been called up and handed their gift bag, Elizabeth asked if everyone was ready for their treats.

"Oh, but wait, I have a few more gifts!" Santa said.

He reached into his bag and pulled out three gift bags. He gave one to Laura, one to Kamie, and then he pulled out a larger one and handed it to Elizabeth.

"Oh, Santa, you didn't have to do that!" She was elated.

Santa crossed his arms. "Didn't you forget something?" he asked.

"Forget something?"

He looked at the kids with a mischievous grin. "Did Miss Bennet forget to say something?"

"Thank you!" they all screamed with laughter.

Elizabeth shook her head with a sigh of remorse. "Santa Claus, please forgive me. I thank you very much!"

The room was filled with shrieks of excitement as they all enjoyed their Christmas goodies and speculated what was in each of their gift bags. Santa remained a little longer, talked to the kids, Laura, Kamie, and Elizabeth, and then said his goodbyes with an added, "Ho, ho, ho!"

The students bid him goodbye with more shouts of "thank you" as Elizabeth turned to him.

"I want to thank you, so much. I don't think I could have hired a better Santa if I had put an ad online and interviewed day and night for two weeks. And thank F&D, as well. Today has been such a blessing."

"I'll do that. Good day, Elizabeth, and have a Merry Christmas."

Kamie walked him to the door to let him out. When she returned, she said to Elizabeth and Laura, "I can't believe I am saying this, but I think I am in love with Santa Claus!"

The three ladies shared a laugh, and Elizabeth ushered the boys and girls to a large round rug and had them sit down. She then told them they could open their presents while Kamie and Laura cleared the table.

Laura brought Elizabeth's gift over to her, which she had left at the table, but she was so engaged watching the joy of the students as they opened their gifts, that it remained unopened in her hands. They received mittens and gloves, scarves, an appropriate reading-level book, dolls for the girls and cars for the boys, and then each pulled out an envelope addressed to their parents. When one child held it up, asking what it was, Elizabeth took it in her hands and could tell it was a gift card.

She shook her head in amazement. F&D had gone above and beyond what she had expected - what she had even dreamed! "Children, these are for your parents, so put them back in the gift bag, and I'll make sure they know to look for them when they pick you up."

Elizabeth looked over at Laura and Kamie, who were ogling their new leather gloves, knitted scarves, and gift cards. She looked down at her gift bag but decided she would open it once everyone was gone.

As the students began playing with their toys or reading their books, the parents began to arrive. The ornaments they had made were placed in the gift bag, and Elizabeth told each parent there was something special for them inside, as well. She didn't know how much their gift cards were for, but her two teachers had each received $100, so she surmised theirs would be the same.

Once the last child was gone and it was finally quiet, Laura and Kamie finished cleaning and then left. Elizabeth slowly walked over to her unopened gift bag.

She picked it up, feeling shivers of anticipation that she had not felt in a long time. She reached in and could immediately tell there were several things inside.

She pulled out a pair of leather gloves and slipped them on her hands, thinking how great they would be on a cold winter day. Next, she pulled out a beautiful, rich, deep blue knitted scarf. She reached in again and felt a small box.

She pulled it out and opened it, gasping as her eyes pooled with tears when she realized what it was.

"What…?" She shook her head as she stared at a prepaid credit card for $1,000.00 that she could use anywhere. Her hands were shaking as she covered her mouth and stifled a sob. "This has been the best Christmas ever!" She let out a laugh. "F&D, I don't know who you are, but I think I love you!"

Chapter 11

February

"How do I look?" Jane asked as she stepped into Elizabeth's room.

Elizabeth looked up after slipping on her shoes and smiled. "You look lovely, Jane, as always."

Jane gave a single nod of her head in her sister's direction. "You look nice, also." She smiled. "You aren't trying to impress someone, are you?"

Elizabeth's brows lowered. "You know that isn't the case. I don't even know why I agreed to go with Will to the theater tonight, except that I want to see this performance, and I hope that having you and Charles along will make it a tolerable evening."

"I wish you would give Will a chance. Charles thinks highly of him and respects his opinions on things."

"I like Charles. I give him two thumbs up, and while Will has certainly displayed kindness and generosity, I'm not totally convinced that he isn't a typical wealthy businessman, whose priority is his job."

Jane smiled. "Well, I am glad you like Charles."

Elizabeth laughed. "How could I not? He came for Christmas dinner and seemed to enjoy the chaos, craziness, and confusion of our whole family being home." She winced. "Especially Mother."

"Yes, but you forgot one word in there."

"What was that?"

"Compassion. He saw the compassion we have for each other." Jane came and sat down on the bed next to Elizabeth. "He told me he could see how we all care for one another."

Elizabeth let out a resigned sigh. "That we do."

"Charles doesn't have that anymore. He and Caroline are not particularly close, and with his father gone and his mother remarried and living in Florida, he doesn't feel he has a deep connection with anyone in his family." She tugged her sister's sleeve. "He told me he wants that in a family of his own."

Elizabeth turned to face her. "He is wonderful, Jane, and I am happy for you. Just don't try to imagine anything between Will and me. We are vastly different from each other, and I'm certain he is not interested in me, either."

Jane gave her a questioning look. "Then why did he ask you to go with him tonight?"

"Most likely because I happened to mention it when he was at PREP installing the computers, and I think he just felt sorry for me."

Jane laughed and stood up. "Believe that if you will, but I choose to believe he asked you because he likes you." She looked down at her watch. "They will be here in twenty minutes. I need to finish getting myself ready."

Jane stepped out, and Elizabeth called after her. "I don't know what else you plan to do. You already look beautiful!"

Elizabeth stood up and walked to the full-length mirror inside her closet door and looked at herself. She was certainly not as pretty as Jane, and she couldn't in her wildest imagination believe that Will had any special feelings for her. A twinge of disappointment swept through her, and she quickly pushed it away.

Precisely twenty minutes later the doorbell rang, and Elizabeth went to answer it. When she opened the door, she was surprised to see that only Charles stood there.

"Hi, Charles. Come on in. I thought you and Will were coming together."

He looked at her sheepishly. "We were, but something came up at his office. He asked me to apologize to you and tell you he would meet us at the restaurant."

"Oh." Elizabeth refrained from saying what she really thought. "That is unfortunate."

"Yes, he…" He was interrupted by the appearance of Jane. "Jane! You look lovely!"

Jane smiled demurely, thanked him, and asked where Will was. As Charles again related Will's excuse, Elizabeth sent Jane an 'I told you so' look.

Later, as Charles drove them to the restaurant, Elizabeth sat silently in the back seat, allowing him and Jane to converse. She could readily see how much they cared for each other, and they seemed well-suited.

The restaurant was next to the civic auditorium, where the musical was being performed. They had reservations and were quickly seated. They ordered their drinks, and Elizabeth wondered if Will would ever arrive. Charles received a text which answered her question.

He read the text: "I'm on my way and will be there in fifteen minutes. Order me the bacon-wrapped filet with a baked potato, steamed vegetables, and a Caesar salad. Sorry."

Elizabeth took a sip of her water and looked at Charles. "Does he often work late? Does he work a lot of hours in a week?"

Charles shook his head. "He is just like his father. When I would go to their house when we were younger, I hardly ever saw his dad home. He always said he didn't want to be like him, but…" He gave a shrug. "When the company was dropped into his lap after his father died, I guess it was inevitable that he would be working as much as he is."

"I see," Elizabeth sent a nod in Jane's direction.

Fifteen minutes later, Will arrived and hurried to the table. "I'm sorry I'm late. Have you ordered?"

"Yes, we just ordered."

"Good!" Will sat down and looked at Elizabeth. "How are you, Elizabeth? Are things going well at PREP?"

"As well as can be expected."

"Good."

Elizabeth noticed he seemed preoccupied and attributed it to not being able to leave his work at work.

Will leaned back as if he was exhausted, concerned about something, or just didn't want to be there. He and Elizabeth were silent as Jane and Charles carried most of the conversation. Elizabeth almost expected him to get a phone call which would take him away from the dinner and theater.

They walked from the restaurant to the theater, and Will finally seemed to be more himself. He wasn't particularly lively and outgoing, which were two traits Elizabeth enjoyed in a person, but at least he was friendly, attentive, and a good conversationalist. He did, however, seem preoccupied. She had seen a livelier side of him at the Gala and when he came to install the computer, but she resigned herself to believe that side of him was not often displayed.

It was the opening night of the performance, and they had excellent seats, in the fifth-row center. The acting, music, and sets were superb, and at the intermission, they had a lot to say about the first half as they walked out to the lobby.

"This play is very entertaining," Charles said. "The characters are all so appealing."

"They are," Will said. "But don't forget the title of the play. '*Hindsight*' indicates things will most likely change."

"I have my suspicions on where the hindsight will come into play, but I won't share my thoughts." Elizabeth smiled conspiratorially. "At the end, I'll you whether I was right or not."

Jane's smile dropped in a pout. "Oh, I don't want anyone to turn out to be bad. I want them all to be happy and live happily ever after."

Charles chuckled and put his arm about her, leaning in. "Isn't she the sweetest romantic and optimist?" He kissed her cheek. "Well, here are the restrooms. Let's meet back here."

They separated to go to the restrooms, and Jane took Elizabeth's arm. "Lizzy, I am so glad to have a few moments alone with you. I am having a wonderful time with Charles, but more than that, having you and Will along." She let out a sigh. "It reminds me of our first date."

They stepped into the line that had formed, and Elizabeth shook her head. "I told you not to get any ideas about us, and after seeing how late Will was tonight because of something that came up at work, it only reinforces what I believe about him."

Jane's shoulders slumped. "I am sure there must have been a good reason."

Elizabeth gave her a resigned look. "There is likely always a very good reason for him to stay at work late." She looked directly at Jane. "You heard Charles. He works long days and almost every day of the week. Unfortunately, it seems he has turned into his father!"

When Elizabeth finished, she told Jane she would meet her back in the lobby and walked over to where they had all arranged to meet. Only Will was there.

"So, do you think you have the whole story figured out?" Will asked with a smile.

"I am not certain, but I have always been a good judge of character, and while these aren't real people, the author normally gives you some hints that will point you in the right direction if you look for them."

Will was not able to respond, as Charles returned.

"Good! It's just the two of you! I have a big favor to ask!"

"What is it?" Will asked.

Charles beamed and looked from one to another. "Will, would you be able to take Elizabeth home tonight?"

Will looked at Elizabeth, who gave a nonchalant affirming shrug, and he looked back at his friend.

"Yes, why?"

Charles clasped his hands. "I would like to have some time alone with Jane. Tonight, I am going to propose to her!"

"Really!"

"Really?"

Both Will and Elizabeth responded in unison, but with different tones and different meanings. While Elizabeth had excitement in her voice, Will's seemed accusatory.

"Charles, are you certain? You have only been dating a little over three months!"

"I've never been more certain of anything in my whole life!"

Elizabeth reached over and touched Charles' arm. "I am very happy for you. I can see that the two of you are perfectly suited." She sent Will a derisive look.

"I hoped you would approve." He directed this to Elizabeth. "Now, please don't say anything to Jane. I want it to be a complete surprise."

When Will didn't say anything, Elizabeth said, "Your secret is safe with us!"

Jane caught up with them, and there was no further conversation on the subject.

They returned to their seats a few minutes before the performance resumed. Will seemed somewhat restless, as he fidgeted and tapped the armrest with his fingers. Elizabeth was grateful she could lose herself in the musical for the next hour or two. Will's response had angered her, and she hoped that he wouldn't interfere with his friend's – and her sister's – happiness.

~~*

When the play ended, they fought the crowds out of the theater. Charles told Jane that Will had offered to drive Elizabeth home, and Jane sent her sister a teasing look. If she knew what had transpired when she was still in the restroom, she wouldn't have entertained such a notion. Charles and Will were parked in a different area, so they bid each other good night. Elizabeth couldn't wait until Jane got home to find out everything that had happened.

Since Elizabeth didn't know where Will had parked, he put his arm about her and drew her close as they waded through the crowd of people. People were taking pictures everywhere, and at one point, Elizabeth was blinded by several flashes. Several people acknowledged Will, and she was amazed to see how many people knew him. Although it shouldn't have surprised her. He probably had come to opening night for several years and had met the same people again and again.

Elizabeth breathed a sigh of relief when they stepped outside into the cool February night, and Will withdrew his arm. She suddenly felt colder, but she wouldn't give any credit to it being Will who had warmed her.

They said little until they reached Will's car. When they both got in, Elizabeth said, "You didn't seem particularly pleased with Charles's announcement that he was going to propose tonight."

Will turned to look at her. "You don't think it's too soon?"

"They're both old enough to know what they want and who they want, and they seem to have found it in each other."

Will was silent for a moment. "I wish I could be as confident as you."

"Look, I know Jane. She is as dear to me as anyone. I wouldn't want her to marry someone who was not right, and I have complete faith that they will do well together." Elizabeth crossed her arms, and as she did, her purse dropped off her lap onto the floor. She heard her keys fall out and scrambled to pick up her purse and keys.

Will tapped the steering wheel. "I am sorry. I should not have reacted as I did. I had something come up at work earlier that completely unsettled me, and I am trying to decide what to do about it."

Elizabeth turned back. "Anything you want to talk about?"

Will let out a soft grunt. "Not particularly. I just want you to know that I do regret how things went this evening."

There was silence again, and then Will asked, "Were you right in your suspicions?"

Elizabeth sent him a questioning look. "Suspicions?"

"About the play – the hindsight in '*Hindsight.*'"

"Oh," she chuckled. "Well, I was right in a few instances, but not all. It was very well-written. The clues were all there, but I didn't see them all."

"I'm glad you enjoyed it."

When they got to the apartment, Will stopped the car and proceeded to get out.

"No, that is okay. You don't have to walk me to the door."

"I know I don't have to." He walked around to her side and opened the door anyway, despite her protest.

"Thank you." As Elizabeth stepped out, she thought he had better not have any intention of kissing her goodnight.

When they got to her door, she pulled her keys out of her purse and turned to him. "Thank you, Will." She turned back, opened the door, and stepped inside before he was even able to respond.

She leaned against the door after she had closed it and shook her head. "Why does he have to be such a workaholic while at the same time be so handsome, gentlemanly, and smell so good?"

Chapter 12

Elizabeth was still awake when she heard Jane come in. It had been difficult for her to fall asleep, as her mind was busy thinking about Charles proposing to Jane and attempting to determine what her feelings for Will were. She heard voices in the other room, so she knew Charles had also come in. She glanced over at the clock and saw that it was after one-thirty. She hoped he wouldn't stay long.

She decided she would sit up in bed and read, knowing that if Charles had proposed – and she was certain he had – Jane would want to come in and tell her. After fifteen minutes, she heard him leave, and she turned off her reading device, waiting for Jane to come to the door.

Jane knocked lightly and whispered, "Lizzy! Are you awake?"

Elizabeth chuckled. "Of course, I am. Come in."

Before she had even finished speaking, the door opened and Jane entered, turning on the light, and promptly sitting down on the bed.

"You won't believe what happened tonight!"

Elizabeth paused before answering, debating whether to admit that she knew, but finally deciding to let Jane have all the joy in making the announcement.

"Charles asked me to marry him!"

Elizabeth let out a squeal and gave her sister a hug. "Jane, I am so happy for you! I hope he knows he has the most beautiful, kind, and generous fiancée that any man could ask for." She tilted her head. "You must tell me how he popped the question."

"Oh, Lizzy. I wasn't expecting it at all! We drove through old town and got out and walked. We went into a little all-night bakery and got a raspberry Danish and coffee, and took them to the park, where we sat down and enjoyed them."

"And did he drop down on one knee?"

Jane smiled. "Not immediately. After we finished, he took his napkin and wiped some powdered sugar off my cheek, and then looked inside the napkin, a look of surprise spreading over his face."

"Surprise?"

"Yes! He had somehow hidden a small box in his hand and as he pulled it out, he slowly lowered down to one knee! Oh, Lizzy, I could barely breathe!"

Elizabeth drew her into an embrace. "Jane, I'm so happy for you!" She suddenly drew back. "You did say, 'Yes,' didn't you?"

Jane laughed and held out her hand so Elizabeth could see the ring. "I most certainly did!"

"It's beautiful, Jane."

"He is going to speak to Father tomorrow. He said he knew he was going to ask me soon, but tonight presented the perfect opportunity with Will driving you home."

"I see."

Jane looked at her with brows lifted. "I was pleased to hear that Will was taking you home. Did you enjoy your time with him?"

What could she say? The only thing they had talked about was their differing opinions on whether Charles was proposing too soon.

"Ah, yes. He was the perfect gentleman."

Jane lifted a brow. "Did he…"

Elizabeth quickly shook her head, giving her sister a warning look. "He walked me to the door, but he didn't come in, and he most certainly did not kiss me goodnight, if that's what you were wondering."

A pout appeared on Jane's face. "I had so wished…"

Elizabeth put up her hand to stop her. "There is to be no more speculation or hope, my dearest sister." She looked at the clock. "Now, if you don't mind, I need my beauty sleep. I know you don't, for you are five times more beautiful than I could ever wish to be. We can talk more in the morning – about you and Charles, not about Will and me."

They hugged again, and Jane stepped out. Elizabeth dropped her head onto the pillow, pulled the blanket up, and let out a sigh.

~~*

The next morning Elizabeth pulled herself out of bed after tossing and turning for most of the night. While she was delighted about Jane's exciting news, it had occurred to her that once the couple married, there was the strong possibility she would see Will more often. She could only hope that her sister would finally see that she and Will were ill-suited for each other.

She got up and began to make breakfast, and soon Jane came out.

"I thought for sure you would sleep a few more hours."

"I smelled bacon," Jane said with a laugh.

"I have the bacon made, and I was just about to make some eggs. How do you want yours?"

"Scrambled is fine," she replied.

"Scrambled it is."

As Elizabeth mixed the eggs and seasonings together, she glanced up. "What are your plans today? Are you seeing Charles?"

"I am, but first he's going to see Father, and then he'll be coming over to pick me up." She chuckled. "Hopefully, he will have good news that Father gave him his blessing for us to marry!"

Elizabeth gave her a pointed look. "Is there any doubt he will?" She laughed. "Father knows he would have to endure the wrath of Mother if he didn't, and she would probably never speak to him again!"

Elizabeth put the eggs in a pan and stirred them as they began to cook. "What are the two of you going to do today?"

Jane shrugged. "We want to start putting together our guest list and wedding registry and talk about our wedding plans."

"Really? So soon?"

Jane looked down sheepishly. "Well, we talked about getting married in three months, so we need to get started."

"Three months?"

"We both think May is a lovely month for weddings."

Elizabeth opened her mouth and then quickly closed it. "You'll have a lot to do in a short amount of time."

"We want a small wedding. I think we'll be able to manage."

Elizabeth let out a puff of air. "Just remember, Jane, no matter how small the wedding is, Mother will make it a big affair!"

"Oh, I certainly hope not!"

Both sisters looked at each other and laughed.

~~*

Later that afternoon, Elizabeth sat alone reading. Charles had come, and she had offered her congratulations to him, especially for securing her father's blessing. Then he and Jane left to begin their day planning for their wedding.

She chuckled to herself, as she concluded that Jane was so accommodating that she would acquiesce to anything Charles wanted. And Charles was so smitten with Jane, that he would agree to anything she wanted. She hoped that one of them would be assertive enough to make the decisions required for the wedding.

She was curious how her parents felt about everything, so she went to get her phone out of her purse to call them. When she reached in to pull it out, she immediately noticed her wallet wasn't in there. She searched the different compartments, and her heart began to race as she wondered what happened to it. Fortunately, the phone was in there, and she just stared at it, trying to recall the last place she had it.

She realized it must have fallen out of her purse in Will's car last night with her keys! Her head dropped back, and she closed her eyes. "No, no, no!" She gave one last desperate search of her purse, and when it turned up nothing, she let out a groan. She knew she would have to call Will and ask him to check the car's front passenger seat for it.

She pulled out the business card he had given her and entered his number. She was grateful when it went to voicemail.

"Hi, Will. This is Elizabeth. I may have… I think when I dropped my purse in your car last night, my wallet may have fallen out. Could you check the front seat to see if it's there? If it is, I can… I will… maybe I can come and get it."

Elizabeth ended the call, dreading the thought of having to see him again – and for her own foolishness. She didn't know whether she wished more that it would be in his car or the restaurant or theater.

When the phone rang, she saw that it was Will and answered it.

"Hi, Elizabeth. I am in my car right now heading to my office, and yes, it is here. I hadn't seen it earlier because it was partially under the front seat. I have a short errand to run, and then I'll bring it by your place."

"I'm grateful you found it, but I hate for you to have to do that. It was my fault and…"

"No, it isn't a problem. As long as you don't need it within the next half hour, I can bring it to you."

"Thank you," Elizabeth said softly. "I appreciate that."

She got up from her chair and began to pace about the room. She wondered whether he would want to bend her ear on Charles and Jane's engagement. Would he be upset everything was heading towards a wedding in just three months?

She sank back down in the chair and picked up her book. No use wondering about it. "Will will do what Will will do." She rolled her eyes and let out a soft moan.

~~*

The sound of the doorbell startled Elizabeth, and she opened her eyes and looked about. She had fallen asleep, and it took her a few moments to remember where she was and what she had been doing. She jumped out of the chair when she realized who was at the door.

"Coming!" she called out as she walked to the door. She stopped at a small wall mirror and looked at her reflection, quickly tidying her hair. She raised her arms in frustration and asked, "Why did I do that? It's only Will!"

She opened the door and her jaw dropped.

"George! What are you doing here?"

"What kind of greeting is that?" He tilted his head and walked in. "I was in the neighborhood."

Elizabeth turned to close the door, hoping she would be able to get rid of him before Will arrived. She readily recalled his warning about the man.

"I'm sorry, George. I just wasn't expecting you." She turned to face him. "How have you been?"

He gave a casual shrug. "I have been better."

"Oh? Why?" She really didn't want to invite him to sit, but he walked over to the sofa anyway. She sat on a chair across the room.

Instead of answering, he pulled out his phone and began scrolling through it.

Filled with impatience, she looked down at her watch. "George, I'm sorry, but I have something I have to do. What brings you here?"

He looked up and held his phone out to her. From her chair, she could only see that it was a photograph. She stood and began to walk over, her chest tightening as she drew closer, and the picture came into focus.

"Where did you get this?" she asked, grabbing the phone and staring down at a picture of her and Will that had been taken at the play the previous night.

George gave a nod of his head. "There are several. Slide through them."

Elizabeth knitted her brows as she looked at the pictures. There was nothing to be ashamed of in them, they had been taken when they were walking through the theater in the midst of the crowd, and he was holding her close so they wouldn't get separated.

Underneath the pictures was the caption, "Handsome Will Darcy, CEO of Darcy Enterprises, was seen last night at the premier of *'Hindsight'* with an unknown lady on his arm. Purported to be one Elizabeth Bennet, it has come to our attention that she runs a daycare center in Meryton Heights."

Elizabeth grumbled and murmured, "It's a tutoring center!"

"So how do you know Will?" George asked, shoving his hands into his pockets. "I only ask because I have concerns about him."

Elizabeth studied his face. He certainly wasn't pleased, which did not surprise her, considering Will's warning to her about him. She wondered about the history between the two men.

"It's very simple, George. Jane is dating his good friend, Charles. In fact, just last night they got engaged. I only went to the play with Will because of that connection." She was frustrated that she felt the need to explain to him, of all people. Her eyes narrowed. "Where did you get these photos?"

"From a website that posts pictures and information about local people of interest."

She asked him pointedly, "And do you frequent these websites?"

George let out a laugh. "Not at all!"

"Then explain to me how you came to know these were posted. These were just taken last night!"

He leaned in towards her. "My mother sent me the link. She is very familiar with the Darcy family, as my father was CFO of Darcy Enterprises, and she knew you from the few times we went out." He gave a shrug. "She was as curious as I was about the connection between the two of you."

"Well, I am sorry to disappoint you, George, but there is no connection other than Charles and Jane." She handed him back his phone.

George lowered his brows. "Are you certain that's all there is?" He scrolled through the phone again.

"Yes, why?"

George handed her the phone again but instead of another photo, there was just text. It was a comment under the picture. Elizabeth's eyes grew wide as she read it.

'Not only was she on his arm last night, but she was also in his arms the night of the Darcy Christmas Gala when he danced the waltz with her, instead of his sister, Georgiana. Who is this lady who thinks she can easily step in and ruin the five-year tradition of Will and his sister dancing the waltz? Tongues were wagging that night, and more were probably wagging after seeing them together again last night. ~CeCe'

Elizabeth felt every fiber in her body tense as she read it. Before handing the phone back to him, she glanced up at the name of the website. She wondered how many people visited this website and what other comments might appear.

"I appreciate your concern, George, and while I'm not pleased that this kind of thing is being posted online about the two of us, there is little I can do. We were not on a date, and there is little likelihood of me going anywhere with him again."

"I'm glad to hear that. Some may think he is all good and generous, but he's certainly not loyal to his family or his friends!" George's face grew distorted in his anger. "I don't normally express harsh opinions about people, but this man is merciless!"

Elizabeth could not contain her curiosity. "In what way?"

"As I said, my father was the CFO, and both he and the late Mr. Darcy had been working with me to replace my father when he retired, which would have been in about five years. When he passed away unexpectedly, Mr. Darcy assured me – no, promised me – that I would continue to get the training I needed to step into my father's shoes. Unfortunately, Mr. Darcy died in a car accident a year later, and Will became CEO. He made it clear in no uncertain terms that I'd never be moving into that position… ever!" George raked his fingers through his hair. "I knew I couldn't work a moment longer under the man, so I quit!"

Elizabeth felt herself grow weak. "I find it difficult to…" She shook her head. "I'm sorry he treated you unkindly."

"Well, I just felt I needed to warn you."

"I appreciate it, George," she said as she ushered him to the door. "It was… it was nice seeing you again, but I have things I must do."

At the door, he turned around. "Are you up for coffee some day?"

Elizabeth shook her head. "I think not, George. I just don't have time."

George slowly nodded. "Let me know when you do."

"Sure. Goodbye, George."

When she shut the door behind him, she turned around and leaned against it. She closed her eyes and blew out a frustrated puff of air.

She walked to her computer and began a search for the website that had posted the pictures, pondering George's words. It was one thing for her to feel a certain way about Will, but it was something else to hear George's accusations.

She found the website easily. It was listed as 'The one place to find all you want to know about the local wealthy, eligible, and beautiful people.' The pictures were posted with the most recent ones first, and since the ones of her and Will were just posted last night, they were still at the top. She scrolled down to read a few more comments that had been posted.

'Who is this Elizabeth Bennet? I had every hope of Will Darcy someday being mine!' There were several heart emojis and then the name *Linny*.

'Sorry, ladies. Looks like Will Darcy is no longer eligible. But I still am!' It was signed by someone using the name *Waiting*.

Elizabeth shook her head, wondering how a photograph of her ever ended up on a webpage like this. She hoped none of her students or their parents would see it.

There was a knock at the door, and Elizabeth stood up. She hoped it had been long enough for George to have left without being seen by Will. She was certainly not in any mood to talk and could only hope he would give her the wallet and leave.

She opened the door. "Hi, Will. Thank you for bringing me my wallet."

She reached out to take it, but instead of handing the wallet to her, he asked, "May I come in?"

Chapter 13

Will handed Elizabeth her wallet and then took quick, long strides into her apartment. Elizabeth could see by both his posture and his countenance that he was tense. She was certain he wasn't pleased and attributed it to the engagement. She presumed he was probably also upset he had to make a special trip to her apartment to return her wallet. She hoped it wasn't because he had seen George.

"Will, I want to apologize for dropping my wallet in your car. I would have been more than happy to pick it up myself."

He waved a hand through the air. "There is no need to apologize. It was no trouble."

"Well, I thank you." She pressed her lips together as she waited for him to speak.

He abruptly turned. "Charles texted me this morning and informed me that Jane accepted his proposal."

Here it comes! Elizabeth thought. She flashed him a triumphant smile. "She did, as I knew she would, and my father gave Charles his blessing this morning. They're already out making wedding plans." She lifted a single brow as if to challenge him.

"Are they? Well, I do wish them well." He shifted from one foot to the other, and his chest rose and fell as he drew in and then let out a deep breath. "Do they know yet when the wedding will be?"

"Yes. They would like to marry in May."

Will's brows lifted. "May? So soon?" He shook his head. "I really don't think..." He paused. "Never mind. It isn't up to me to decide these things for them."

Despite having the same reaction regarding how soon their wedding would be, it angered Elizabeth when Will expressed the same sentiment.

"I hope they will be happy."

By the look on his face, his posture, and the tone of his voice, Elizabeth didn't believe he truly felt that way.

He began to rub his jaw. "Elizabeth, last night was a disaster in more ways than one, and I apologize for it. I was greatly disturbed by some things that came to light at work, things that are yet to be resolved, and I wasn't the best company. My attitude was abominable."

"Yes, you explained that last night."

Will looked intently at her. "I would like to make it up to you. You deserve better than the way I treated you. Next month, Georgiana and her boyfriend are using my pair of theater tickets themselves, but I would very much like you to join me for the showing in April, '*Singing in the Rain*.' I would…"

Elizabeth put up her hands to stop him. "Will, you are certainly under no obligation to try to make up for last night." She let out a huff. "It is completely unnecessary."

"I am not asking you out of obligation. I am asking you because I am... the times we have been together have been..." Will began to pace around the room and then stopped. "Elizabeth, you must realize that I am very fond of you, admire you, and I would very much like for you to go with me to the theater... as my... date."

Elizabeth drew back. "Your date?" She froze for a moment and then repeatedly shook her head. "I… I thank you. I'm flattered, but…" Her throat was dry, and she swallowed hard. "I'm sorry, but I don't think so."

Will's eyes were fixed on her, and he gave her a questioning look. "Are you busy that night… or do you not want to see that particular musical?" He paused. "I would very much like you to accompany me."

"Will, you and I are… we are completely different. Despite living in the same city, we live, work, and are friends with people who are from two completely different worlds."

Will looked down, and his brows lowered. He muttered something unintelligible.

"But it isn't only that."

Will's eyes shot up and he felt his chest tighten.

"You are the type of man who puts his job and company before anything else, having very little concern for your family, friends, or even your employees." She crossed her arms.

Will glared at her, and his expression seemed a mixture of anger, incredulity, and… something else. Was it disappointment?

"Is this truly what you think of me?" He raked his fingers through his hair.

Elizabeth was speechless. She had not been expecting this at all. They'd certainly had some enjoyable times together. She had even begun to see him in a different light, but to begin a dating relationship with him was unthinkable.

"It pains me to say this, but… the position you hold in your company, your responsibilities, and your demanding work schedule is…" She paused. "I just don't think I want to be part of that life." She neglected to mention his wealth, but that was something completely different.

Will was silent for a moment, and he began to pace about the room again, as if attempting to determine what more to say. He suddenly stopped in front of the computer and noticed the picture on the screen. He turned back to Elizabeth. "What is this?"

She walked over and let out a soft gasp when she realized what he had seen. She quickly recovered, however, and gave him a pointed look. "This is yet another thing!"

He gave his head a shake. "Were you doing a search for me on the internet, or does this just happen to be a website you regularly check?"

"Heavens, no, to both! Someone just informed me that pictures of the two of us had been posted on this website. I couldn't believe it when I saw them."

"If this is what has you upset, it'll soon be forgotten. I can guarantee that once pictures of someone else have been put up, these pictures will be history."

"Until the next time it happens." She let out a long sigh. "Will, these pictures of us aren't the main reason for my feelings, but I was certainly not pleased these were posted online. What if the families I work with see this? And my students? Many of these families can barely make ends meet and don't know where their next meal will come from! And here I am traipsing around with a millionaire with seemingly not a care in the world."

"Elizabeth, I would hope that my monetary worth doesn't define or change who I am." He began to scroll through the pictures. "And there is nothing improper with any of the pictures themselves, and they can certainly find no fault with you going to the theater with me."

Elizabeth's shoulders dropped. "You are right. It is just that I was surprised they were here for all the world to see. Some of the comments are…" She gestured towards the screen and watched Will read the comments, frowning as he did.

He stood up and turned to face her. "I'm sorry this has upset you. It is something I've had to get used to, and I have learned to pay it no heed."

She watched him in silence for a moment. She could see he was wrestling inwardly about something. He finally spoke.

"I assume it was George Wickham who informed you about the pictures?"

Elizabeth was taken aback. "I…"

"I saw him leave when I pulled up. Is he the one who told you about the website and the pictures?" He looked at her intently as he waited for her to answer.

Elizabeth drew her shoulders back and returned his gaze. "As a matter of fact, he did." She nodded her head for emphasis. "He wondered how we knew each other."

"He wondered, did he?" Will shook his head. "I have often questioned what the man does in his spare time but following this website would have never entered my mind."

"He wasn't the one who found it online. Apparently, his mother saw them, and she asked him how you and I knew each other."

"His mother!" He looked back at the computer screen and then back to Elizabeth. "Well, that I can understand. She is… well, never mind."

"George said he has some concerns about you."

"Oh, he did, did he?"

"He claims you passed him over for a position that your father had promised him."

Will's jaw dropped as he looked at Elizabeth incredulously. "Do you always believe the claims of someone with such questionable character?"

"Questionable character? I've never seen anything in his character that I would deem questionable." Elizabeth paused as she attempted to gather her thoughts. "Do you deny that you passed him over for a position promised to him? A position he was being

97

trained to step into?"

"If I did, I had my reasons."

"Yes, I'm sure someone in your position can toss out any number of reasons to justify whatever you choose to do." She attempted to rein in her anger. "Will, you've been very generous to me and to PREP, and I do appreciate that. But from our very first encounter, I knew I could never date someone like you. I didn't want to then, and I certainly don't want to now." She drew in a long breath. "I am sorry to speak so frankly, but I truly cannot consider dating you!"

Will stood silently for a moment. He turned and began walking to the door. He opened it and stopped, looking back at Elizabeth. "You have certainly expressed your decided opinion of me and have left me with no misunderstanding regarding your feelings. Forgive me for having taken up so much of your time. I wish you well, Elizabeth."

When he walked out the door, instead of feeling a wash of relief, Elizabeth was stricken with a surprising wave of grief. Tears came to her eyes, which she quickly wiped away. She had done what she had to do. She told him what he needed to hear. Then why was she feeling this way?

~~*

As soon as Will closed the door behind him, he paused and forced himself to draw in a breath. He narrowed his eyes as he pondered what had just happened.

He loosened his fists, which were so tight his nails were digging into his palm. He took quick, long strides away from the door and began rubbing his jaw. He could not determine whether he was angrier at George Wickham, Elizabeth, or himself.

"No!" He came to an abrupt stop. "I did nothing wrong. I won't apologize for the success of the business my grandfather began." He began walking again and muttered under his breath, "But George Wickham is another story."

Chapter 14

May

Elizabeth stood back to admire Jane in her wedding gown.

"My dearest sister, you're the loveliest bride I've ever seen." She drew close and wrapped her arms about her.

"Oh, Lizzy, you're too kind. I just wish I wasn't so nervous."

"It's normal to be a little anxious on a day like today." Elizabeth squeezed her and leaned back. "Nothing will go wrong, and if it does, as long as the two of you are married at the end, it is of no consequence."

"But I so want it to be perfect."

Elizabeth stepped back and crossed her arms. "I'm sure it will be." She let out a soft laugh. "If anyone messes up during the ceremony, my money would be on Will. I can't believe he didn't make it to the wedding rehearsal yesterday."

"He said something came up at work," Jane offered softly.

"Well, if you ask me, things come up at his work far too often."

Jane reached out and took her sister's hand. "It shows he cares about his company."

Elizabeth shook her head. "It shows he cares more about his company than his family and close friends!"

"Lizzy, I doubt that is true."

"How can you say that when he doesn't show up to the rehearsal, and then doesn't come to the dinner until we are practically finished?" She pressed her lips tightly together. "I just hope he shows up on time for the wedding!"

"I'm sure he will. Whatever kept him yesterday was likely very important."

"As I'm sure it was also important the night we went to dinner and the theater. He continues to sink in my estimation."

Jane let out a sigh. "I wish you could see how good a person he is." She looked up and smiled. "Guess what he's going to do?"

Elizabeth tilted her head. "I have no idea."

Jane leaned in with a look of eager anticipation. "He offered to drive us to the hotel after the reception in a classic convertible his family owns."

"Really? A classic convertible? When did this all come about?"

"We have known for a while. He didn't want anyone else to know that it would be our getaway car in case someone got the crazy idea of decorating it by writing something silly on the car and windows while it was in the parking lot."

"Like Kitty or Lydia?"

Jane nodded.

"That was very kind of him to offer to do that," she conceded. "Leave it to him - or to his family - to own a classic convertible." She paused and reached for her sister's hands. "Jane, I'll admit I have seen good in him, but his priorities, his... his dedication to his company, while admirable, takes up too much of his time, and that's not something I want in a partner."

"Just be kind to him."

Elizabeth propped her hands on her hips. "I have always... for the most part... been kind to him." *But today I will try to avoid him as much as possible to make it easier*, she thought to herself. *Especially considering the last time we were together. He will likely want to stay as far away from me as I want to be from him!*

Elizabeth looked at her watch. "Now, my dearest Jane, it's about time to go out. Do you have everything you need?" She tilted her head. "Any final touch ups?"

"No, I think I'm ready."

"Good! Let me find Charlotte and ask her whether everyone is in the chapel. Then I will make sure Father is ready. I'll be right back."

~~*

Jane, Elizabeth, and their father stood at the back of the chapel waiting for their cue to walk in. Charlotte Lucas, the wedding coordinator, peered through the small window in the doors watching and listening. Charlotte was a close friend of Jane and Elizabeth, who, at the age of twenty-seven had never married, but found great enjoyment and fulfillment acting as everyone else's wedding coordinator.

She stepped back and opened the door. "Elizabeth, you may now walk down the aisle. No need to rush; you have plenty of time. Just as we practiced last night."

"Thank you, Charlotte."

Elizabeth stepped out in her seafoam mid-length halter gown and smiled at the small gathering of family and friends turning their heads to watch her walk towards the front. She carried a small bouquet of peach, yellow, and white flowers. When she lifted her eyes, instead of noticing Charles, she noticed Will.

She was startled to see him, not because she thought he wouldn't show up, but because she had forgotten how handsome he was when dressed in a tuxedo, as he had been at the Gala. She had to force herself to look at Charles, whose eyes were fixed on the doors.

Elizabeth smiled when Charles finally looked down at her, and she could see that he was nervous, too. She gave him a nod of encouragement. Her eyes drifted to Will, again, and she gave him a forced smile before stepping into her place.

When the wedding processional commenced, and the doors were opened, Jane and her father began to walk towards them. Elizabeth thought she looked like an angel, gracefully floating on air in her high-waisted ivory satin gown with puff sleeves and delicate lace around the neckline. Elizabeth smiled at her sister and then glanced at Charles, who was beaming. At his side, Will was looking at her instead of Jane. She felt her cheeks warm and quickly turned her attention back to her sister.

When Jane came up and took her place next to Charles, Elizabeth reached down to straighten her gown and train, took her bouquet, and then turned back with all of them to face the pastor, who began the ceremony.

Charles and Jane recited their vows to each other, and the pastor gave a short message about love from the book of 1 Corinthians 13 in the Bible. He gave a charge to the couple to love, honor, do their best to obey, and to quickly forgive each other when they didn't, which prompted a chuckle from the guests. They exchanged rings, and then they were pronounced husband and wife. They kissed and walked arm in arm back up the aisle.

Elizabeth and Will stepped towards each other, and she lightly slipped her hand in his extended elbow. She barely touched him and refused to look at him. She couldn't wipe his presence completely from her mind, however, due to his cologne. Why did he have to smell so good?

When they passed through the doors, Will looked down at her. "Elizabeth..."

Elizabeth interrupted him. "Excuse me, Will. I would like to stop in the restroom before they call us back for pictures." She said it as politely as she could and turned to walk away. She hoped that once the pictures had been taken, that would be the extent of her having to deal with Will Darcy.

When she came out of the restroom, she walked back to the chapel to see the guests had just finished leaving, so she stepped back in. The photographer was giving some directions, saying he wanted to photograph the family first, so they could then leave and join the guests at the reception. He would then photograph the wedding party, which consisted of Charles, Jane, Will, and herself. Finally, he would take pictures of just the bride and groom.

Elizabeth entertained herself by watching Caroline Bingley, who continually smiled at Will, sat near him, and tried to engage him in conversation. It was apparent she really liked him. A thought suddenly came to her. Could Caroline be the CeCe who posted a comment on the website? Or perhaps Linny? She shook her head, rolling her eyes as she considered this.

She couldn't help but try to assess Will's response to the woman's undivided attention. By his solemn expression, it appeared he wasn't as interested in her as she was in him.

When all the family pictures had been taken, her family, as well as Charles' mother and stepfather hurried out to join the guests in the reception hall. Caroline left somewhat reluctantly.

Elizabeth then joined Charles and Jane, along with Will, for the wedding party pictures. The photographer took several photos and poses of them, and Elizabeth was grateful she was always positioned next to Jane, while Will stood on the other side of Charles.

When they were excused so the photographer could take pictures of just Charles and Jane, Elizabeth offered to remain back to make sure Jane's dress and train were laying right for each photo. She smiled at her brilliant idea as she watched Will walk out alone.

Once the photographer was satisfied with all the pictures he had taken, they proceeded to the reception. An archway, decorated with flowers and ribbons, was placed at the door. Will was waiting just inside, and when Charles and Jane were ready, Will signaled to the DJ to announce them. Everyone stood and applauded when they came in through the arch.

The room looked beautiful. The tables had been decorated with centerpieces of candles in goblets, surrounded by ivy and baby's breath, and woven with ribbons. Each place setting had little lace bags filled with candies. The wedding cake was on a table in the corner, and long tables lined the room filled with an array of foods for everyone to enjoy. The guests had already begun to eat.

They walked up to the main table set apart for the wedding party and parents of the couple. She sat on Jane's side between her sister and their parents.

During the meal there were the traditional toasts offered to the new couple. Following that, there was the cutting of the cake, and finally the tossing of the bouquet and garter. Elizabeth could care less about catching the bouquet, but she knew Jane had every intention of throwing it in her direction. She had determined that even if it landed right at her feet, she wouldn't make any attempt to grab it.

There were about ten single ladies gathered for the toss. Before turning around, Jane looked directly at Elizabeth and smiled, prompting her to give her head a quick shake back at her.

Jane tossed the bouquet high in the air, and as Elizabeth surmised, it came right at her. She did a side-step away as Lydia came flying towards her, knocking it away. The bouquet landed directly in Mary's hands.

Elizabeth laughed and let out a cheer for Mary, while Lydia let out a frustrated cry. But it was the disappointed look on Caroline's face that really made Elizabeth smile.

Later, when Will caught the garter, she was certain that Caroline was even more disappointed, for had she caught the bouquet, in her mind that would have been all that was needed to ensure an engagement and marriage between the two.

Later, the lights were lowered as the DJ asked the bride and groom to come out and dance their first dance as husband and wife.

It was just dusk, and the lights in the room made their dance magical. When they had finished, the DJ announced the bride and groom would dance with her father and his mother.

Tom Bennet eagerly stepped out to dance with his eldest daughter, while Mrs. Bingley joined her son on the dance floor. Elizabeth could readily see that both parents were a bit emotional. It was a touching sight.

With Charles and Jane on the dance floor, there was no one between Will and herself, as he sat to her left. Elizabeth looked about for an excuse to move away. Noticing her aunt, Maddy Gardiner, she walked over to her. "Aunt Maddy, are you enjoying the wedding?"

"I am. The ceremony was lovely." She turned to watch the dancing couple. "It appears they are very happy."

"I think they are, and they seem to be well-suited for each other."

Maddy looked at her niece, giving her a pointed look. "And when can we expect another wedding?"

"Oh, Aunt, I don't have the time to even consider anything like that."

Maddy looked at the head table. "The best man is certainly handsome."

Elizabeth let out a huff. "Yes, handsome, but a workaholic if I ever saw one." She let out a chuckle. "He didn't even make it to the wedding rehearsal yesterday and barely made it to the dinner."

The music came to an end, and Elizabeth applauded softly, along with everyone else.

"Charles and Jane think highly of him, but I really want nothing to do with him."

The DJ announced that there would be one more dance before everyone would be invited onto the dance floor. This dance would be for the bride and groom, their parents, and the best man and maid of honor.

Elizabeth gasped. "No! Jane didn't say anything about this!" She looked over at Jane, who looked just as stunned and gave a slight shrug.

"Well, my dear, he is walking over and doesn't seem at all

surprised.”

Will came over, extending his hand. “I believe this is our dance.”

Elizabeth said nothing, trying to figure out how this happened. Her aunt reached out and took his hand, giving it a gentle shake as she introduced herself.

“It is a pleasure to make your acquaintance.”

Maddy nudged Elizabeth gently. “Enjoy your dance, Lizzy.”

Elizabeth could think of nothing that would give her less pleasure.

She glanced up at Will. “I know you must be just as surprised as I am by this dance, and are probably just as unhappy about it as I am. I am certain the DJ must have made a mistake.”

“No,” Will said. “It was not the DJ’s mistake.”

“It wasn’t?” Elizabeth asked.

“No. I asked him to include us in the dance.”

Chapter 15

Elizabeth's head shot up, and she glared at him. "This was your idea? You asked him to announce a dance that included the two of us? Why would you do such a thing?"

"Don't worry, Elizabeth. I am not going to press you again to accept a date from me."

Elizabeth's brows lowered. "Why, then, did you do it?"

"I felt it would be the only way I would have some time alone with you and could tell you what I need to tell you."

The music began, and Will placed his arm about Elizabeth's waist and took her hand in his. She slowly and lightly placed her other hand on his shoulder.

"Now, I would ask that you try not to look alarmed by what I'm going to tell you. Keep smiling so as not to alert the other guests that you are distressed."

"Distressed?"

Will tilted his head. "Keep smiling, Elizabeth."

She sent him an exaggerated smile. "What is it you have to say to me?"

Will blew out a puff of air. "I wanted to explain why I was late yesterday, as well as the night we went to dinner and the theater."

"You already did. Something came up at work."

"Yes, but back in February, I had just learned from an audit we had done that someone in our company had absconded with at least one hundred thousand dollars."

Elizabeth drew back in shock. "One hundred thousand…?"

Will nodded. "Keep smiling."

"Do you know who did it?"

"Back then, no. But just yesterday we were able to narrow down how it was done. That is why I was absent from the rehearsal and late to the dinner. We now also know for certain who the perpetrator was."

He looked down at her and squeezed her hand. "This is where I would ask that you not react and just keep smiling."

Elizabeth did not need to hear him say the culprit's name. She knew who it was.

"It was George Wickham," Will said softly. "I am sorry to have to break the news to you."

Elizabeth's mouth went dry, and she felt herself grow weak. "I would have never imagined he would do something like this." She looked up at him. "Are you quite sure?"

As if he knew his support was needed, his hold on her grew firm. "Even I am surprised by his actions, but even more surprised that he had been able to do it in a way that took us so long to discover it. It wasn't easy finding out who was behind it, but I became suspicious when I saw George that day at your apartment. He got into a car that was worth considerably more than he could ever afford."

Elizabeth looked up at him. "I thank you for telling me, but I want to assure you there is nothing between George and me and never has been. We went out on a few dates, but that is all." There was a tremor in her voice, and she hoped he wouldn't perceive it as something it wasn't.

"I'm glad, but I also need to ask you to keep this confidential. The evidence is being accumulated, and an arrest will probably be made some time this next week. Once he is arrested, it will be common knowledge, and you will be free to talk to others about it."

Elizabeth looked down. "I understand. I will keep it to myself."

"Thank you. I knew I could trust you." His hand gently squeezed hers.

She was touched by his trust in her. "He told me he quit the company because you wouldn't consider him as his father's replacement as CFO, as your own father wanted." She looked up with a pained look on her face. "I imagine he figured out a way to take the money in retribution and made his exit with it."

Will's face darkened. "Please allow me to clarify something. He didn't resign; he was fired. I did not make him CFO because of his character. He wasn't the type of person I wanted as an executive of Darcy Enterprises. I am sure my father would have felt the same way." He shook his head. "And from what we've now discovered, he had been pocketing the company's money for at least six years."

"Even before your father passed away."

Will silently nodded.

"I see."

They continued to dance in silence; Elizabeth's feelings were in a turmoil. Strangely, she no longer harbored resentment towards Will. He had been through a lot, taking over the company when his father died, and then this. However, she still felt his responsibilities as CEO ruled his life.

When the dance ended, Will stepped back. "Thank you, Elizabeth. You need not fear that I will intrude upon you again." He gave her a quick smile and turned to walk away.

Her parents caught up with her as they walked back to their seats. "My, that young man is so handsome!" her mother exclaimed with a broad smile.

"Now, my dear," her father said. "Let us not have such wishful imaginings regarding our Lizzy." He turned and winked at his daughter. "Will Darcy is rich, to be sure, but he likely has an army of women vying for his attentions."

"But Tom, the two of them looked quite lovely together, and I couldn't help but notice how engaged they were in conversation with each other!" She laughed. "Even you commented on it!"

Elizabeth put up her hands. "I will have no more of this. Will and I will never be a couple, so you can just put that little thought out of your combined heads!" She fought back the tears that were threatening to spill.

"But why?" her mother asked.

"He is… he is very different from me. He often works too many hours a day for my satisfaction." Elizabeth's shoulders slumped. "He is a good man in a position with a lot of responsibilities, and that will affect every part of his life."

"My dearest daughter," Mr. Bennet began, "Think of all the times you have stayed late at work or gone in on the weekend because something came up." He sent her a pointed look.

"That is different," Elizabeth weakly protested, knowing it was true. The very thing she accused Will of doing, she did herself.

"But if only you had caught the bouquet. I doubt that Mary..."

"Mother, please. Catching the bouquet means nothing other than trying to figure out what to do with it once the flowers have died."

Elizabeth was grateful for the diversion her parents provided for her, even though it centered around Will. Her argument to them reinforced what she needed to hear herself. She could only hope she sounded convincing.

For the remainder of the evening, Elizabeth kept herself busy avoiding Will. It was not difficult, as Caroline was almost always at his side.

As the time grew near for the newlywed couple to depart, Elizabeth noticed Will walk out. Jane came over and asked her to accompany her to the restroom.

When they walked in, Jane reached out and took her sister's hands. "Lizzy, I want to thank you for everything! I can't believe that..."

Elizabeth leaned over and kissed her cheek. "You can't believe you are married? Well, I can! And you have a wonderful husband,"

"Thank you." Jane cast her eyes down and then looked back up. "I'm sorry about the dance. I think the DJ must have been confused."

Elizabeth gave her a reassuring smile. "You need not worry, Jane. It is over and done."

"You and Will were talking quite a bit."

"Yes, but as I said to Mother and Father, it was nothing. I warned them not to get any ideas about us."

"You look sad, Lizzy. Is something wrong?"

Elizabeth looked at Jane, forcing a smile. "Nothing is wrong, unless you consider I'm losing my favorite sister who's also my best friend, and I'll no longer have someone waiting for me to get home safely each day."

Jane chuckled. "I will put an app on my phone that tracks your location just so I can make sure you are home safe each day."

Elizabeth drew her into an embrace. "I will miss you, Jane, but I'm am also so very happy for you." She could feel her eyes moisten with tears.

"I will miss you, too!"

They joined Charles, who waited to escort Jane outside, where the guests were waiting to send them off.

Mary, Kitty, and Lydia had passed out small vials of bubbles to the guests, and some were already filling the air with them. As the couple made their way through the crowd, cheers and more bubbles flooded the area.

When Elizabeth saw Will in his car, she gasped. It was a beautiful classic convertible that appeared to be from the forties. It looked brand new, other than being an old model. No wonder he didn't want anyone writing on it. He looked very handsome in it, and Elizabeth had to remind herself of all the things she didn't like about him. Having Caroline standing at the driver's side talking to him helped.

She felt a hand on her shoulder and turned to see her aunt. "That is a nice car, isn't it?"

"Yes, it is."

"It is too bad he is so disagreeable to you. I thought the two of you made a very nice-looking couple as you danced."

Elizabeth turned to her. "As I told Mother and Father, do not get any ideas about us." She put up a finger as if scolding her. "And I don't want you putting any additional ideas into their heads!"

"I wouldn't think of it."

Charles helped Jane into the car, they turned and smiled for a few pictures, and then waved. Jane blew a kiss in the direction of the guests but fixed her eyes on Elizabeth.

Elizabeth smiled, holding back tears.

Caroline finally stepped away, and Will turned towards the well-wishers, his arm slung over the car seat. Elizabeth felt her cheeks warm as she met his gaze. He gave a quick nod of his head and then turned to face the front.

Elizabeth was surprised by the dismay that swept through her, and a single tear slid down her face.

Her aunt put her arm about her. "Things may have changed today, Lizzy, but you will soon discover that your deep love and affection will remain as strong – or grow even stronger – than it has ever been."

She leaned her head on her aunt's shoulder as she watched the car – and Will – pull away. She knew her aunt had been talking about her relationship with Jane, but she couldn't help but think it more strongly described how she now felt about Will Darcy.

Chapter 16

The Following December

Will rose from his leather chair and walked to the window. He stood with his hands tucked casually in his trousers' pockets as he gazed out at the grey sky, wondering when it might begin snowing. It was cold enough. From the 7th floor of his office building, he could readily see people below bundled up with coats, mittens, and scarves, hurrying about as they tried to finish their Christmas shopping before the projected snow began falling. Despite being only two o'clock, the gaily lit decorations from the shops and street below twinkled brightly, a sharp contrast to the dreary day.

He walked to his office door and slowly opened it. He peered out, meeting Mrs. Reynolds' eyes as she immediately looked up.

"Yes?" she asked, but then looked at the phone when it rang.

He shook his head and waved for her to take the call.

He waited to see if the call was for him. He heard her say, "Good afternoon. Darcy Enterprises. This is Mrs. Reynolds." After a pause, she asked, "Do you want to…" and then she stopped. She didn't say anything else except muttering an occasional 'yes' or 'no.'

When it was apparent that he wasn't needed, he turned to gaze out at the large office before him. Despite most of the employees having left for the day, there were still signs of that afternoon's Christmas party. A decorated tree stood in the far corner, complete with empty boxes wrapped in cheerful Christmas paper beneath. Its branches were adorned with festive ornaments and strung with blinking colored and white lights. Various Christmas decorations still rested upon desks, now vacant, and a table was strewn with remnants of the catered lunch. Those few employees who remained were eating some of the leftovers as they finished up their work. He could just barely hear the music playing. Someone had put on a variety of Christmas music, and he heard a little bit of everything, from classical to modern rock songs. He was glad the day was over, and he would enjoy two weeks of peace as everyone enjoyed their Christmas break.

He had never felt like Scrooge before, but this past year his world had come crashing down around him. Three months ago, his beloved grandmother had passed away. She had been the thread that held everything and everyone in his family together. With her gone, the Christmas Gala, which had been just a week ago, had lacked something. His aunt and uncle had taken charge and had made several changes. He had not been pleased.

And then there was Elizabeth Bennet, who had told him emphatically – and quite vehemently – she had no interest in dating him. While that had been several months ago, he was still reeling from her accusations and strongly worded dislike of him.

He now seemed to have little reason – or desire – to celebrate the holidays.

Upon reflection he had realized Elizabeth's accusations – some of them, anyway – had merit. He had wrongfully voiced his concern over Charles and Jane's engagement. And yes, he did tend to put his work before relationships. He didn't like it, but that was part of his job. When he met Elizabeth, it was the first time he truly wanted to make someone a priority in his life, but he found that he didn't know how to go about it. He was so entrenched in every aspect of his business that he found it difficult to let things go.

And now, despite being acquainted with her feelings for him, he was ready to do that very thing – let things go. He wondered if it was too late.

She had been wrong about George Wickham, however. At least Will had been able to explain to her what that scoundrel had done. She would have eventually found out, as his arrest made the local news outlets and was also being picked up on certain internet sites.

Will had found Elizabeth so lively and genuine; he had wanted their relationship to work. His grandmother had said she was authentic and to not let her get away. Unfortunately, Elizabeth had claimed he was the last man in the world with whom she would want to be in a relationship. He blew out a frustrated huff.

Will knew he could attempt to explain himself to Elizabeth. He had considered writing a letter, emailing, or texting her, but every time he began, he sounded defensive. He wanted to justify his actions and how she perceived his character, but in the end, he decided to let it go. Unfortunately, he found it very difficult to let *her* go. As a result, he threw himself even more into his business, effectively bringing his social life to a standstill. Not that it mattered; there was little that seemed appealing to him.

He shook his head. He and Elizabeth were too different, like opposite sides of a magnet. He was corporate America, living in an expensive townhouse in an upper-class part of the city, and working 60-80 hours a week. While he knew most of his office staff, he didn't know them intimately. He communicated with them mainly through his valued assistant, Mrs. Reynolds.

Elizabeth, on the other hand, was director of a tutoring facility for underprivileged children. She had two employees who enjoyed working for her and helping when they could. They were still in college, and while getting their degrees, Elizabeth gave them practical experience in child growth and development.

Family was important to her, and she spent a lot of time with them – particularly Jane, with whom she was very close.

Mrs. Reynolds finally ended the phone call with, "Thank you, and Merry Christmas and Happy New Year to you."

Will turned and looked at her questioningly.

"I think the employees enjoyed the party today, Mr. Darcy. I'm sure everyone appreciated you coming by and presenting their Christmas bonuses, which, of course, delighted them."

Will nodded, noticing that she ignored the fact he attended the party only briefly. Idle conversation with people he wasn't close to was not his strength. He found it difficult to share in the festive Christmas spirit that everyone else seemed to have – that he *normally* had.

Even though the employees had been given two weeks off, he would spend most of those days in the office, until he joined Georgiana at his grandmother's – now his aunt and uncle's – home on Christmas Eve. They would spend Christmas Day together with extended family.

He recollected the call Mrs. Reynolds had just taken. "Who was on the phone?"

"It was your cousin, Richard."

"Oh. Why didn't you give me the call?"

"He is sick. He could barely talk. He just wanted me to convey some information to you."

"What is it?"

She looked up at him as if reluctant to reveal the matter.

Will pressed his lips together as he waited for her to continue.

"Richard was supposed to play Santa at the PREP Christmas party this afternoon. Obviously, he can't do it with his cold."

Will's heart gave a sudden lurch at the reference to Elizabeth's tutoring program. He thought a man his age wouldn't suffer love pangs, but he did at just the slightest mention of her.

She tilted her head and smiled. "He would have called earlier, but he hoped he would feel better by this afternoon. Unfortunately, he seems to be worse."

"Is there anyone else who could do it?" he asked.

Mrs. Reynolds looked out across the office as the last employees walked out the door. "Well, I think everyone here has left." She smiled. "You know I'd do it in a heartbeat, but I don't think I would fool the children one bit – even with a pillow under the suit, the long white hair, beard, and moustache."

Will covered his mouth with his hand and stood silent for some time as he contemplated the situation.

"I will… I will find someone," Will stammered.

Mrs. Reynolds smiled. "The Santa suit is here in my office, along with all the gifts." She eyed him knowingly. "It isn't that difficult to play Santa, you know. All you have to say is, 'Ho, ho, ho' in a deep voice. We even have thick white eyebrows and facial glue to keep everything firmly in place!" The way she looked at him, Will knew she felt strongly that he should do this. "No one has to know who you really are… that is, that you are not really Santa Claus."

Will took a deep breath and held it while he examined his options. At last year's party, Elizabeth had only known that a man from F&D Foundation named Richard had come dressed as Santa bringing a bag filled with gifts. Her staff greatly appreciated that the company took such an interest in helping them have a merrier Christmas. They had no idea who had been behind it, and he wanted to keep it that way!

"No need to worry, Mr. Darcy," Mrs. Reynolds said with a wave of her hand. "If you can't find someone to do it, we can just pack up the toys and have a courier deliver them. I know the children will be disappointed that Santa himself was unable to come, but they'll soon forget that when they get their gifts in their precious little hands." She looked at him over the rim of her glasses.

Will raked his fingers through his hair. "I'll figure something out."

"I know you will!" Mrs. Reynolds quickly assured him with a smile and a glimmer in her eyes. "Now, Santa is supposed to be there at four o'clock, which will be here before you know it." She pointed to a box in the corner of her office. "Everything is there, including the Santa costume and accessories and the bag of presents. I assume you don't need directions."

"No, I…, no."

"Splendid!" Mrs. Reynolds gave a clap of her hands. "Oh, and one of our lawyers – that is, F&D's lawyers – called Miss Bennet today and gave her the news about the possibility of a building being available for PREP to move into if she wants. He said she was overjoyed and so grateful."

"I am glad to hear it." And he was! Now Elizabeth wouldn't have to worry about closing her doors when the city began construction of the new convention center. He had been determined to find something else for her and he had found the perfect place. "Thank you for all you have done, Mrs. Reynolds."

"It is always my pleasure, sir. Merry Christmas."

"Thank you. I hope you and your family have a very merry Christmas, as well."

"Thank you, sir. I just have a few more things to do, and then I am gone." She began to turn back to her desk but stopped. "Oh, and Mr. Bingley called while you were at the party. He left you a message on the office line.

"Thank you."

Will returned to his office, collapsing into his chair. He was tired and wasn't certain what he would do about PREP's Christmas party. Could he face Elizabeth again? He decided he would listen to the message from Charles, first, and then decide what to do.

As he listened to his friend's message, his jaw dropped.

"Hi, Will. This is Charles. I wanted to tell you something Jane told me. I don't know if this is at all pertinent to you, but the other night at the Gala, there was a couple there by the name of Goulding. I don't recall ever seeing them there before, but I know there were a lot of new people because your aunt and uncle are now in charge."

Will's brows furrowed, and he wondered what the Gouldings may have done to cause Charles to call him.

"Jane told me that this couple's son was involved in a fatal car accident that killed one of Elizabeth's students, and because of their wealth, their high-priced lawyer got him off, and basically turned things around, so much so that the mother now blames herself for her daughter's death, when it was clearly the Gouldings' son's fault. Anyway, Jane said Elizabeth now has a difficult time trusting people with money."

Charles said a little more, but Will's mind reeled with this revelation. This was the family whose son had killed Elizabeth's student! No wonder she resented him and his wealth.

When the message ended, Will stretched out his arms and placed his hands firmly on his desk, narrowing his brows as he considered what he was about to do. He stood up and walked into Mrs. Reynold's office just as she was gathering her things to leave.

"I have decided that I will go today as Santa."

Mrs. Reynolds clasped her hands together. "Oh, I know you'll be perfect!"

"I doubt that, but I will give it a try."

Mrs. Reynolds again wished him a very Merry Christmas and Happy New Year as she walked out. He wished her the same.

He returned to his office and sat down. Opening his desk drawer, he pulled out a small box. As he closed the desk drawer, he asked himself, "What did I just get myself into, and more importantly, what will Elizabeth think if – and when – she finds out Santa is me?" For an inexplicable reason he found he didn't care and looked forward to it with a surge of anticipation.

Chapter 17

At three thirty, Will walked out of the building carrying a bottle of water for himself and the bag of gifts for everyone at PREP. He had already donned the Santa outfit and hoped no one would see him – or at least recognize him – as he walked toward his car. When he was almost there, he suddenly stopped.

It was probably not wise to drive his luxury car to that part of town, especially when dressed as Santa. Besides, Elizabeth might recognize it. He shook his head. Did he really think he could carry this off and have her *not* recognize him?

He jingled the keys in his hand and fingered through them, finding the key for the company car, which was parked next to his. He unlocked the trunk and placed the bag of gifts inside. Shutting it firmly, he opened the car door and climbed in.

He looked around the dashboard of the car, reacquainting himself with it. It had been a long time since he had driven it. "Probably time to replace it," he said aloud, as he remembered it lacked most of the newer cars' amenities.

As he drove through the busy streets towards Meryton Heights, he took the time to mentally prepare himself to see Elizabeth again. But could he emotionally prepare himself? If the nervous churning in his stomach was any indication, it was a futile attempt.

Occasionally he noticed people looking at him and pointing. He encountered a variety of reactions from people who saw him in the Santa suit but found himself smiling when a child waved excitedly. He was surprised how easy it was for him to wave back. He also rehearsed saying, "Ho, ho, ho." He tried several different voices and finally decided upon the one he would use. He was certain Elizabeth wouldn't recognize it as it was deeper than his normal voice. He glanced up at his reflection in the mirror and hoped the disguise was good enough that she wouldn't recognize *him*, either. Or did he really hope she *would*?

When he finally pulled up to the old brick building, his chest constricted. He had been here just once, and that was a year ago, but he had pleasant memories of eating and talking with Elizabeth.

He parked the car, and before getting out, he looked into the rear-view mirror. He pressed his thick white eyebrows and moustache to ensure the glue was still sticking and that they covered, along with the beard and long flowing curls of the wig, most of his face.

He stepped out of the car and straightened the suit, plumping up the pillow and adjusting the big black belt.

He walked to the trunk and opened it. "Ho, ho, ho," he said as he pulled out the bag of gifts. "Ho, ho, ho," he said again as he closed the trunk. He drew in a long breath. "Here I go!"

He walked up to the door, which was decorated with a fresh wreath. He rang the bell, and after a brief wait, a voice came through the intercom.

"Yes?"

He paused, not knowing what to say. Finally, in his deep voice he said, "Ho, ho, ho! It's Santa Claus here for the party."

"Good!" an unfamiliar high-pitched female voice exclaimed. "We have been expecting you! Come on in."

A buzzer indicated that the door had been unlocked and he walked in. He was met by a young lady who introduced herself. "Hi. I'm Kamie." She tilted her head. "And you are *not* Richard!"

"Of course not. I am Santa."

The young lady chuckled. "Follow me. I'll show you where to go, Santa."

As they walked down the hall, she said, "We received some good news today. We thought we would have to close our doors here because of the new convention center being built. Elizabeth has been so worried!"

"But something good happened?" he asked, feigning ignorance.

"Yes! We were told today that a company is offering to help raise funds to purchase a building for us that will give us more space and allow us to have more children in our program. We need to look at it first, but it sounds perfect."

"I am glad to hear that."

He followed Kamie into the large meeting room. He looked around and saw a tree decorated with handmade ornaments – most likely made by the students.

His eyes scanned the room. The boys and girls were gathered around a table and were drawing on a large sheet of paper. He continued his perusal of the room until his eyes finally landed on Elizabeth. She was seated next to a young girl who appeared to be quite upset. Elizabeth combed the girl's hair with her fingers as she spoke softly, trying to soothe her.

Elizabeth suddenly looked up and her eyes widened with joy as she saw Santa. She turned the little girl so she faced him and pointed. "Look, Sara. Do you see who is here?"

The sight of Elizabeth arrested him, and he seemed to lose all his peripheral vision. He was solely focused on her and didn't see the swarm of kids descending upon him.

When he felt the crush of the children against him, his hands went instinctively to protect his beard from being pulled off. There was no need; he towered above them.

Elizabeth immediately called them away from their guest and gently reprimanded them for behaving so disrespectfully. She walked towards him and extended her hand through the throng. "Hello, Santa. It's so good of you to stop by and visit us when I know you are so busy!" A wink to him, while innocent, made him almost forget what he was doing.

Will's mouth went dry at her proximity, but fearful of discovery, he let out a boisterous, "Ho, ho, ho!" He could think of nothing else to say.

Elizabeth smiled, and Will's heart ached. He wished her smile was meant for him, instead of the man in the Santa suit.

"We have a special place over here for you to sit." She pointed to a chair and then gave directions to the children. "Now, all of you must be on your best behavior. Get in a line and when it's your turn, you can sit on Santa's lap and tell him what you want for Christmas." She looked back to him and whispered, "Richard couldn't make it?"

"He is sick." Will shuddered when he realized he had used his regular speaking voice. He hoped she didn't recognize it.

"I'm sorry. I hope he feels better soon. I'm going to be in the kitchen getting the treats ready."

Will nodded and watched with disappointment as she walked away.

He reluctantly turned his attention to the two teachers who directed the boys and girls, sometimes placing them on his lap or holding their hand if the child seemed nervous. The teachers helped distribute the gift bags to each child when they finished. They were told not to open them until they had all received them.

Most of the students approached him quickly, sat on his lap, told him what they wanted, and then hopped down. A couple of them truly tugged at his heart as they told of wanting their mom or dad or brother or sister to be released from prison for Christmas, or their brother or sister to stop using drugs. Some wore tattered clothes that were either too large or too small, and some were too shy to utter a single word. He found himself talking gently to these children, hoping to persuade them to tell him what they wanted, while frequently glancing towards the kitchen door. Each one seemed delighted to receive their gift and responded with an enthusiastic, "Thank you!"

~~*

Something nagged at Elizabeth's thoughts while she hurried to get the snacks ready. She shook her head as she remembered her surprise when she learned about the possibility of a new facility for the tutoring center. The new location was only three miles away, was larger, and would allow her to expand, which she had always wanted to do.

She smiled as she thought that it would be safer, too, since it was located right next door to the division police headquarters. She chuckled at the thought that Jane would be delighted and wouldn't have to worry about her anymore.

As she finished putting ice cream on the last piece of cake, Kamie walked in. "The kids are almost through the line. Did you notice this isn't the same Santa as last year? I'm sorry it isn't Richard, but this guy has the most gorgeous brown eyes."

Elizabeth laughed. "I did notice it wasn't Richard but hadn't paid any attention to his eyes." She let out a laugh. "Chances are you would be disappointed if you saw the rest of his face."

"I would love to see what he looks like without that beard!" She let out a sigh. "And oh, does he smell good! I am pretty sure he is wearing Ardently cologne."

Elizabeth jerked her head. "Ardently? Are you sure?"

Kamie nodded. "My brother wears it."

Elizabeth's hands began to shake. "Kamie, would you mind taking these out to the table?"

"Sure."

As Kamie took the plates, Elizabeth walked out and looked at Santa as he patted the last child's head. He glanced up at her and started to stand, but she lifted her hand. "I have not had my turn yet, Santa. I have a Christmas list, too, you know." Fighting nerves, she walked over to him, and sat down on his knee. She could readily smell the familiar scent that she had come to associate with Will. She looked into his eyes, recognizing the intensity in them she had often seen, yet she couldn't fully comprehend how this could possibly be him. Was it just her imagination? Wishful thinking? No, it *was* Will. She wondered how involved he had been in all of this.

"Are you not going to ask me what I want?" she finally asked.

He was silent for a moment. "Ho, ho, ho!" His voice cracked. "And what do you want for Christmas?" he asked in an odd mixture of Santa's deep resonance and his own mellow voice.

It took a moment for Elizabeth to respond. Her heart pounded as she tried to make sense of this. "I would have said, a new facility for our tutoring center since we must be out of here by the middle of next year when the city is scheduled to break ground for the new convention center. But we just received word that a facility has been found and is being offered to us if we want it." Her voice softened. "But then, you already knew that, didn't you, Will?"

He opened his mouth but did not reply.

Elizabeth leaned in towards him, whispering emphatically. "I don't know how you are involved in all of this, so I am asking you to please remain until after the party when we can discuss this matter privately."

~~*

Will did as he was told, all the while wondering whether Elizabeth would lash out at him with the same fury she had when she had thrown her accusations at him earlier this year. For the remainder of the time, all he could mutter was an occasional, "Ho, ho, ho," and attempt to read the expression on her face when she glanced in his direction.

He wasn't certain how she'd discovered it was him. It had been all he could do to ask her what she wanted for Christmas, let alone do it in Santa's voice. He was certain she suspected it when she came and sat on his lap. He gave his head a slight shake. As much as he enjoyed it, it had also been tortuous having her so close, yet so far from the closeness he wished he had with her!

The parents soon arrived to pick up the children, and Will – as Santa – wished them a Merry Christmas as they walked out. Once the last one was out the door with their gifts, Elizabeth told her two assistants they could leave. They argued that they would help her clean up, but she insisted. Laura and Kamie gathered up their belongings, as well as their own gifts. As they left, Will noticed the looks that passed between them and Elizabeth.

When he heard the door close behind them, Will turned to Elizabeth. "Look, I know how this…"

Elizabeth put up her hand. "Please, Will, before you say anything else, would you do me a favor and please take off the Santa outfit?" A smile escaped her lips. "It makes it very difficult for me to say what I want to say with you looking like that."

"Gladly!" Will began removing the suit and facial disguise. Once it was all removed, with an occasional, "Ouch!" as he pulled off the brows and mustache, he looked at her apologetically. "I'm sorry if I upset you. I can only imagine what you're thinking."

"You have no idea what I am thinking, Will. But I will tell you what I am wondering! Why did you feel that you couldn't let me know of your involvement in this? I suspect F&D is some part of Darcy Enterprises. Am I correct?"

A sheepish look appeared. "Something like that. At least, the D is for Darcy."

"And it was you who asked Richard to pose as Santa last Christmas, provided all those gifts, and now are willing to purchase a facility for us to move into if it suits our needs?"

Elizabeth began to absently pick up the empty paper plates and cups from the table. Will did the same.

"I didn't think you would accept it from my company, knowing how much you dislike me."

Elizabeth looked up at him. "Will, there may be many CEOs

that I dislike, but that does not mean I will refuse their money if they wish to support PREP." She stared at him silently for a moment. "Besides, I don't dislike you."

Will started. "You don't?"

Elizabeth shrugged and said, "At first I did, but ever since..." She paused. "It has been difficult to think poorly of you when all I ever hear from Charles and Jane is praise for you."

"They are too kind."

After clearing off the table and making sure the leftover food was put away, Elizabeth said, "I think that is good enough." She looked at Will. "Would you walk me to my car?"

Will smiled, feeling a little less apprehensive. "I would be happy to, but would you first like to see what your gift is?"

Elizabeth glanced down at the bag on the table and then looked back up at Will. "I know that whatever it is, it is probably too much." She shook her head. "Last year's gift was..."

He picked it up and handed it to her. "Open it later at home, then, if you are more comfortable."

She smiled. "I think I will."

Will picked up the Santa suit, stuffing it into the now empty toy bag, and they walked to the front door. He held it open for Elizabeth, and as she stepped out, she suddenly stopped, saying, "Oh, look! It's snowing!"

She turned and looked at Will. "You don't have a coat on!"

He shook his head and smiled. "It is rather difficult to put on a coat over a Santa suit."

"I would imagine. Do you have one in your car?"

He nodded, and then they stood silently for a few moments. Finally, Will said, "You know, I really enjoyed the party. The boys and girls are amazing."

Elizabeth drew in a deep breath. "Yes, they are."

Will watched as the snowflakes drifted down, several resting on Elizabeth's face and dark hair. He tentatively brushed some away with his finger. "How did you know it was me?"

Elizabeth shook her head. "If you had truly wished to remain unknown to me, you shouldn't have worn Ardently cologne."

He pinched his brows together. "I never suspected my cologne would give me away."

They laughed as they walked to Elizabeth's car. She unlocked the door and turned to face him when he opened it for her. "Thank you for doing this. It meant a lot to the children. And I am sure the facility will be perfect – especially being located next to the police station." She let out a breathy chuckle. "Jane has always been concerned for my safety down here, and I can't help but wonder if you were, too. It makes me wonder just how much you had to pay someone to move out of that place so we could have it."

"I will never tell!" Will smiled and then shook his head. "No. Trust me, it used to be a gym that relocated and has been vacant for quite some time." As Elizabeth slipped into the car, he began tapping his fingers on the door frame.

"Tapping your fingers was always a sign there was something else you wished to say," Elizabeth said teasingly. "What is it?"

Will swallowed; his throat was suddenly dry. "Do you think, would you consider – in the near future, possibly after the holidays – going out for coffee or something… with me?" He winced, held his breath, and waited.

Elizabeth pouted and twisted her mouth. "In the near future? I don't know, Will…"

"Well, I just thought I'd ask. I understand."

Elizabeth narrowed her eyes and looked up at him, making quotation marks with her fingers. "I think in the near future sounds far too vague. How about tonight? Do you have any plans? I'm hungry. All I have eaten today is Christmas party snacks. There is a little café near my apartment that is so cheerfully decorated for Christmas with lights and a big tree filled with sparkling ornaments." She tilted her head. "Are you still in the Christmas spirit after having to endure an afternoon playing Santa?"

Will rapped his hands on the top of the door. "I have not been more in the Christmas spirit this whole season! I can think of nothing I would rather do!"

"It's called the Wooden Spoon, on the corner of Chestnut and 2nd. I'll meet you there."

He watched Elizabeth drive away, grateful for all the joy of the Christmas season that had poured back into him. He wasn't sure how things would turn out with Elizabeth, but he was thrilled that he was going to have a second chance to find out.

Chapter 18

As Elizabeth drove to the café, she felt an elation she had not felt in a long time. She had been more intrigued than captivated with Will when they first met a year ago, but she soon began to see things in him that she considered red flags, things that reinforced her determination to dislike him. She thought he was arrogant, a workaholic, and was certain he placed his job above family and friends.

She shook her head. But ever since Jane and Charles had married in May, she had begun to hear more and more about him and the reasons he was the way he was. Charles was convinced he spent so much time at work because he had no one to come home to, and once he found the right person, that would change. Elizabeth wasn't sure she was willing to find out if that was indeed the case, but after what he did for her this afternoon, she might be willing to give him a second chance.

Elizabeth arrived at the restaurant, surprised at how quickly the time had passed driving over. She rolled her eyes as she realized how focused her thoughts had been on that enigma of a man rather than where she was going. "I'm still trying to figure him out!" she said to herself with a resigned laugh. "Nothing has changed!" She couldn't help but remember her aunt's words to her as he sat in the car to drive Charles and Jane to their hotel.

She had said, *Things may have changed today, Lizzy, but you will soon discover that your deep love and affection will remain as strong – or grow even stronger – than it has ever been.*

Her aunt had been talking about Jane, but Elizabeth's thoughts had gone immediately to Will. Could it be that she had already fallen in love with him all those months ago?

"Merry Christmas, Lizzy!" the waitress greeted her when she walked in. "I have an empty booth over there, if you like."

"Thanks, Melody. Oh, and another person will be joining me."

"Your sister?" she asked.

"No, a gentleman."

Melody's brows lifted in delight. "Wonderful! The usual to drink?"

Elizabeth nodded and then looked about her and smiled as she took in all the Christmas decorations. Garland was strung around every window, column, and counter. White lights attached to the garland twinkled merrily. A large Christmas tree was decorated with both store bought and handmade ornaments. A small Christmas village was set up in the center of the café, and a miniature train chugged around it, its soft whistle occasionally mixing with the Christmas music playing in the background. Large red and green candles were lit on every table, and the flames seemed to dance to the music. The smell of cinnamon and clove permeated the air.

Elizabeth walked over to the table and took off her coat, laying it over the seat. A bell rang as the door opened, and Elizabeth turned to see Will walk in. Melody hurried over to him.

"Good evening, sir," Melody said. "A party of one tonight?"

He saw Elizabeth, giving a nod of his head in her direction. "Actually, I'm with her."

As he walked over to her, Melody's eyes widened, and she sent Elizabeth a nod of approval.

He took off his overcoat and placed it on the booth's bench.

When Will sat down, his phone rang, and he pulled it out to answer it.

Elizabeth waited patiently as she listened to his conversation, feeling somewhat apprehensive that maybe things would still be the same with him.

"What? Really? I had my phone turned off earlier. All right. I'll see you in a few days. Thanks for letting me know. Same here. Bye."

Elizabeth was surprised when he put his phone away. She'd assumed he would leave it out on the table as so many people do.

"I apologize for that. I needed to take the call." He looked about. "They certainly go all out with decorations," Will said.

"Yes. It is very festive."

Before Will could respond, Melody brought over a steaming mug and placed it in front of Elizabeth. She handed them both menus and then asked Will, "What would you like to drink, sir?"

Will opened his mouth, trying to decide what he wanted. He finally asked, "What does she have?"

"It's our hot spiced apple cider," Melody replied.

"I always order this, especially when it's cold outside." Elizabeth said with a laugh. "Melody doesn't even have to ask me what I want."

"I'll have one, as well."

"I'll be right back with it and then take your order."

Will watched Melody walk away, and then he opened the menu. As he began to peruse it, he asked, "What is good?"

"Everything." Elizabeth clasped her hands and placed them on top of her unopened menu.

"It looks like you already know what you want. Do you always get the same thing?" he asked, nodding to her closed menu.

She shook her head. "No, but I pretty much have the whole menu memorized.

"So… what are you going to order?"

Her lips parted in a wry smile, and she slowly shook her head. "I will tell you only after you decide for yourself. I don't want to sway your decision."

Will's brows narrowed. "I am perfectly capable of making up my own mind. I just wondered."

Elizabeth watched him read through the menu, finally closing it, and looking up. "All right, I have made up my mind. What are you getting?"

She chuckled. "You tell me first."

"I'm going to try the tomato basil and bacon soup in a sourdough bread bowl." He crossed his arms across his menu. "We had a Christmas party at the office today, so I'm not particularly hungry."

"Well, that is a good choice." She leaned towards him and smiled. "I am getting their portobello mushroom burger."

Will raised an eyebrow. "Are you now a vegetarian?"

Elizabeth laughed. "No. I just love those thick slices of grilled Portobello mushroom that taste almost as good as a big juicy hamburger." She shrugged. "Maybe even better."

They sat in silence for a while, and then Elizabeth said, "Will, again, I want to thank you for… for everything. I know the children and their parents will enjoy all the presents."

"It was nothing… but speaking of presents, I have something for you." Will reached into his pocket.

"You already gave me something! I mean, F&D gave me some really wonderful gifts. This is completely unnecessary."

Will pulled out a small box, and Elizabeth eyed it suspiciously. It looked very much like a small jewelry box.

"Go ahead and take it. You'll understand once you open it."

Elizabeth reluctantly took the box but covered it with her napkin when Melody came over with Will's hot apple cider. She took their dinner orders and stepped away.

Elizabeth's heart raced as she looked down at the box. He certainly wouldn't be so presumptuous as to give her a ring! She willed her fingers to stop shaking as she lifted the lid, and then pulled away some tissue paper.

Her eyes shot up. "Will!" Tears formed in her eyes as she looked down at the necklace with the camphor glass pendant. "This was your grandmother's necklace. I was so sorry to hear she passed away. Jane told me."

Will pressed his lips together. "When she became ill, she tucked this into my hand and said she wanted *you* to have it when she was gone. She was too weak to explain why, but I thought maybe you could enlighten me." He briefly looked down. "I wasn't even certain I would have the opportunity to give it to you. I doubted our paths would cross again."

Elizabeth leaned back, looking down at the necklace. "I complimented her on the necklace at last year's Gala. I thought it was one of the most interesting and beautiful pieces of jewelry I had ever seen. She explained to me about camphor glass." Shaking her head, she asked, "But shouldn't this have gone to your aunt or to Georgiana?"

Will looked down as he wrapped his hands about his mug. "Neither of them wanted it. I must be honest and tell you it isn't particularly valuable. The filigrees around the pendant are pure gold and white gold, but only a small amount. And the diamonds, while real, are… well, you can see how tiny they are."

Elizabeth smiled. "I love it!" She let out a sigh. "I wish I could have thanked her." She reached up and put the necklace on. "She told me she always wore it at Christmas because the camphor glass reminded her of a frosted windowpane."

Will looked up and met her eyes. She wondered if he was thinking of their waltz, much like she was.

They continued talking on general subjects until Melody came with their food. "One Portobello mushroom burger for you, and one tomato basil and bacon soup in a sourdough bowl for you." She clasped her hands. "Is there anything else I can get either of you?"

Will sent Elizabeth a questioning look. "Would you care for anything else?"

"This is plenty for me."

Will looked at Melody. "Thank you, but no."

Elizabeth watched as Will took a sip of his soup. "How do you like it?"

"It's very good, and so is the cider."

Elizabeth took a bite of her burger, wiping her mouth as some of the juices dripped down her chin. "Before I ordered this, I should have considered how messy I would get eating it." She let out a nervous laugh.

They enjoyed their food and had almost finished when Elizabeth finally said, "I have to say I have never been more surprised in my life, finding out there is some sort of connection between you and F&D, and then hearing about a possible purchase of a building for PREP." She leaned in towards him. "You know I can never pay you back. It's very generous of you, but worth far too much to just give to us."

Will drew himself erect in the seat. "It isn't as generous of me as you think. The building will not be purchased by me or one of my companies."

"But aren't you associated with F&D? I assume that is why you showed up today as Santa."

Will made a slight wince and began tapping his fingers on the table.

She sent him an inquisitive glance. "You are tapping again. Would you care to explain?"

Will began to rub his jaw. "F&D Foundation is a dream that my cousin and I have had for many years." He paused and smiled. "Richard, who was last year's Santa, is my cousin. He has been looking into all the financial and legal aspects of what we want to do, and things were just about to get going when you and PREP came along."

"I see." She paused and lowered her brows. "Well, I don't really see. What exactly does that mean?"

Will took in a long breath. "With all my acquaintances in the corporate world, and many of them desirous of donating to worthy charitable organizations, Richard and I wanted to start a foundation that would research those smaller organizations, non-profits, ministries, and worthy charities. We would match them up with the larger corporations, finding ones that suit their overall vision statement and be something they would want to contribute to."

Elizabeth opened her mouth but said nothing.

"You became our first recipient." Will looked down sheepishly and then looked back up. "Unbeknownst to you."

Elizabeth shifted nervously in the chair, uncertain how she ought to feel about this.

Will continued. "Richard and I funded last year's party, and he did a little investigating while he was there. Asking innocent questions, getting a feel for what you did… that kind of thing. Your two workers were very helpful in providing him with the information he needed."

"Ahh! My valuable assistants Laura and Kamie! And what, exactly, did he do with that information?"

"In short, he wrote up a profile on PREP, and he began looking at properties that might suit your vision and desire to grow, and then…" Will began tapping his fingers again on the table, but quickly stopped when he realized it.

Elizabeth glanced down at his hand and smiled. "Just say it, Will. No need to worry about my reaction."

"He contacted corporations and presented his report to them, and three of them are interested in helping to fund the purchase – if you find the building and location to your liking."

Elizabeth could barely breathe, and she quickly wiped away a threatening tear. "Thank you. I am extremely grateful."

She noticed that Will seemed uncomfortable with the praise. He was no longer eating his soup, but instead, he was looking down at her burger.

She took the opportunity to change the subject. "Are you not going to finish your soup?"

"Eventually. It's very good, but as I said, I ate a lot today. I was just thinking that Portobello burger looks delicious!"

"It is!"

"I think I'll have to order it the next time we come here."

Elizabeth's head shot up. "Excuse me? Now, wait a minute. What makes you think we are going to come here again – together?"

He gave a casual shrug. "I don't know. You actually seem…"

She tilted her head. "Pleasant? Friendly?" She gave him a teasing smile. "It is the Christmas season, after all."

"You don't seem as angry at me as you have been in the past, and you invited me to join you for dinner tonight."

"Ah. Well, I was hungry, and… after all you've done, it was the least I could do."

"So, what do you think?"

"About us coming here together again?"

He nodded, looked down at his soup, and took another sip. He lifted hopeful eyes to her.

Elizabeth folded her arms and placed them on the table. "Before I agree, do you mind if I ask you some questions?"

"Go ahead."

"First, I must know…" She looked down and drew in a long breath. "At last year's Christmas Gala, was my bid for the computers really the highest?" She looked up hesitantly. "Or did someone else place the highest bid and decide to give the computers to me?"

Will pursed his lips and began to tap his fingers on the table.

Elizabeth reached over and covered his hand with hers. "I believe you just answered my question. That one, at least."

"Let's just say it was done in the spirit of what F&D would do." He tilted his head. "Next question?"

"Gladly. How is it you are forming another company when you already work eighty or so hours a week at the family business?"

He paused before answering. "Charles must have said something, didn't he? He is always telling me I work too hard."

"He has mentioned to Jane how concerned he is that you work so many hours. Is that true?"

Their conversation was interrupted by Melody. "Have you saved room for dessert?"

Both shook their heads.

"One check or two?"

"One," Will said.

"Two," Elizabeth said at the same time.

"Make it one check, please." Will's tone of voice indicated he would not brook disagreement.

When Melody left, Will looked at Elizabeth. "Now, where were we?"

"You were about to tell me whether or not you work eighty hours a week."

"Ah, yes." He took a sip of his cider. "Not always, but yes, I have, and it is something I have vowed I will not continue to do."

Elizabeth gave a derisive laugh. "Starting another company is certainly not the way to cut your hours."

Will finished his soup, pushing the bowl away from him, and crossing his arms on the table. "No, but leaving my position as CEO at Darcy Enterprises is."

Elizabeth gasped. "Leaving?"

"I have already told my uncle and the board of directors to begin looking for my replacement in the new year."

Elizabeth leaned back against the booth and for the first time since coming in tonight, felt relaxed – and rather joyful.

"Do you remember the musical we went to see?" Will asked.

"'*Hindsight*?'"

"I don't want to be like the people in that play who made wrong choices based on their perception of what was before them and found out too late it wasn't what they really wanted."

Elizabeth tilted her head. "Like being CEO of Darcy Enterprises?"

"That and other things. Sometimes things aren't as appealing as you once thought they were." He gave a shrug. "I will still be involved, but only as a board member."

Elizabeth looked down and studied the remnant of the portobello burger on her plate. Without glancing back up, she said softly, "And we also saw in the play, there are times we judge something as being undesirable, only to find out – possibly too late – that it isn't." She lifted her eyes to Will. "A person, for instance."

Their eyes locked, and Elizabeth was amazed – and disheartened – at how wrong she had been about the man sitting across from her.

Will was silent for a moment and seemed to be debating whether to say something. Finally, he said, "Elizabeth, you have a passion for what you do and can share your vision with anyone and everyone. I heard from people at last year's Gala who were quite impressed with you and your tutoring center. You ought to be out speaking about it, raising interest, and encouraging people to come and work alongside of you." He gave a shrug. "Currently you have two very capable employees, and if you want to grow and make your dream come true, you need to go out and make PREP known. You do love to talk about PREP, if I am not mistaken."

"I… I do love to talk about PREP to people, but I never thought I could do both."

"You wouldn't need to give up one for the other, but I believe you could – and should – begin going out and speaking about what you do." Will gave a shrug. "People can also come alongside of you with financial support." He paused, and then added, "But it is up to you, of course. I would never presume to tell you what to do."

Elizabeth smiled, contemplating all he said.

Will's phone rang, and Elizabeth waited for him to pull it out and answer it. When he didn't, she looked at him with surprise. "Are you not answering it?"

He shook his head. "I have the important people in my life set to distinctive rings. Whoever this was can either leave a message or call me back later."

"And that first call?"

"It was Georgiana."

Elizabeth looked at him questioningly. "Is there something wrong?"

"She wanted to tell me that Richard's family has some sort of emergency and will be flying out to California for a couple of weeks. We were supposed to go there on Christmas Day, but they are letting everyone know to make other plans."

"I am sorry to hear that. Will you spend Christmas at the house in Pemberley Estates with your aunt and uncle?"

Will shook his head. "No, they are already in Florida."

"What do you think you'll do?"

He pursed his lips and looked down. "I suppose Georgiana and I will go out to eat somewhere. There are several restaurants serving Christmas dinner." He looked up. "We've done it before."

Elizabeth bit her lip as she considered this. She couldn't imagine spending Christmas without her family. She had no idea what he would say to her next words, but she felt she had to at least offer. "No, I won't hear of that. You will celebrate Christmas with us."

Will drew back. "Who – exactly – is us?"

"My family, of course. Join us at my parent's house. Jane and Charles will be there, as well as our three younger sisters, our aunt and uncle and their kids. It will be chaotic, noisy, and crazy, and you never know what to expect, but it will be fun."

"I… uh…"

Elizabeth pinched her brows. "If you want to harbor even a ray of hope that there will be a second meal here with me, you and your sister will come. Be there around one o'clock. We'll have already opened our family presents, but I may just find something for you and your sister to open. We will eat dinner at three." She gave him an encouraging smile. "What do you say?"

"What can I say?" He laughed. "It seems as though this Christmas is turning out to be unlike any I have ever had."

Elizabeth smiled and placed her napkin on the table. "I hope that's a good thing."

Will looked down at her hand and reached across the table, taking it in his. "So far, I think it's a very good thing, but I do have a question for you."

Elizabeth's brows lifted. "Yes?"

"Do you think you are able to look past my wealth and business to see me for who I am? Charles told me about the Gouldings and how their actions have tainted your view of those with money."

Elizabeth sat silently for a moment. "I… yes, I was quite prejudiced against you for that very reason." She looked down and then back up. "Now, no…not now, but even earlier this year, I began to see you for the man you really are." She sent him a pleading look. "Can you ever forgive me for how I treated you?"

Will smiled. "I most certainly can."

Melody brought the check over, and Will paid it. As they stood up and put on their coats, Elizabeth felt a surge of hope course through her. She knew she and Will were so very different from each other, but the feelings that were surfacing for this man were unlike anything she'd ever felt before.

Without saying a word, they both walked over to the miniature Christmas village and stood quietly as they watched the train circle around it. Elizabeth sighed. "There is something fascinating and mesmerizing about this. Even the sound of it is magical."

The train's whistle blew, and Melody walked past, nudging them both and pointing to something above them.

They looked up and realized they were standing beneath a sprig of mistletoe. They looked at each other, and their eyes locked, but not until after noticing that everyone in the café was looking at them and smiling broadly.

Someone yelled, "Go on! You know what you're supposed to do!"

Elizabeth rolled her eyes, but a smile teased at the corner of her lips.

Will lowered his face towards hers. "You won't slap me?" he asked softly.

A soft chuckle escaped. "There is only one way to find out."

He cupped her chin with his fingers and gently pressed his lips to hers. The kiss was over practically before it began, but it left Elizabeth breathless. She felt her cheeks warm as she looked up into Will's smiling face.

As they walked out, Elizabeth looked up at him. "Why did you feel you had to keep it a secret last year that you were involved in providing the Santa and gifts for our party?"

Will shook his head. "I didn't want you to feel obligated to go out with me because of it." He paused. "I have to confess that I have admired you ever since you uttered those words, 'It is not *Snobs* on the Hill' when we met outside the restaurant that night."

Elizabeth shook her head. "It was terribly wrong of me, and I have to confess I wasn't in the best mood that night."

They paused outside the door and watched as a few snowflakes drifted lazily down.

"It is beautiful," Elizabeth said. "There should be a good covering of snow by morning."

"Would you like me to follow you home?" Will asked.

Elizabeth shook her head. "No, I'll be alright."

Will said no more, and they walked quietly to Elizabeth's car.

When they reached it, she turned and gently fingered the lapel of Will's coat. "I must warn you, Will, that spending Christmas with my family might prove to be your undoing."

"I'll take that risk."

Elizabeth smiled as she unlocked her car and then turned back to him. "I can't thank you enough for everything, Will. For your generosity in finding us a new building, for being Santa for the children, for the computers, for joining me for dinner, and for…"

When she said no more, Will tilted his head. "If you're going to thank me for anything, thank me for the kiss."

His eyes penetrated hers, even in the darkness.

"It could hardly have been called a kiss." Elizabeth laughed and hoped Will had not detected the tremor in her voice.

His arms suddenly went around her, pulling her close, and she looked up at him with a mixture of expectation and nervousness. Before she could think of anything to say, he kissed her again, this time more soundly. She wrapped her arms about his neck, holding him tightly, not wanting him to stop.

He slowly drew back and touched his forehead to hers. "Are you going to slap me for that one? After all, there is no mistletoe."

Elizabeth let out a breathy chuckle. "You are certainly taking risks tonight."

"It was a risk I would readily take again – and it was quite worth it!"

She shivered, and he held her tighter. "Are you cold?" he asked.

"Not at all."

She leaned her head against his chest, enjoying the warmth and the sound of his heartbeat in her ear. She finally pulled away. "I ought to be going. Thank you again, Will."

"I'll be counting down the days until Christmas, Elizabeth."

She turned and stepped into the car. Before she closed the door, she looked up and said, "I want you to know, Will, that I will be counting down the days to Christmas, too!"

Chapter 19

Christmas Day

Elizabeth stood with Jane at the kitchen sink in their parents' home washing the dishes from their traditional Christmas morning breakfast. Sizzling bacon, fluffy scrambled eggs, and delicious homemade cinnamon rolls had been devoured by everyone. The Bennet family then gathered to open their presents.

The three younger sisters had been home two weeks, and Charles and Jane had come that morning just in time for breakfast. Their aunt and uncle and young cousins would be arriving closer to noon, and Will and Georgiana a little later.

Their father and mother had been elated when Elizabeth told them that Will Darcy and his sister would be joining them. In addition to their mutual delight, their father had been surprised, and their mother had become anxious about having such an illustrious man from a wealthy family come to their modest home. Elizabeth continually reassured her that she had no reason to worry. Even this morning, as her mother got the turkey ready to put in the oven, she began to question everything she did, even though she had prepared the turkey effortlessly for many years.

When the two eldest sisters were alone in the kitchen, Jane looked at Elizabeth as she placed a dish in the dishwasher. "I know you have heard me say this many times already, but Charles and I are delighted that you and Will seem to have settled your differences." She lifted her brows. "Do you think we can hope for something more to come of this?"

Elizabeth looked both ways to make sure her mother was not in hearing distance, and then she chuckled. "Don't let Mother hear you say anything she might construe as Will and me being in a relationship. We're going to take things one day at a time, but I... I do hope so."

Jane closed the dishwasher door and started it running. She then looked up beseechingly. "Charles and I are convinced you and Will are perfect for each other."

"Well, I must admit that everything I have seen of him, and the changes he is making in his life, are all good indications of how I might come to feel for him."

She looked towards the family room, where Kitty and Lydia were laughing at something, and their mother was scolding them to keep quiet. "Today will be a good test to see whether Will wants anything more to do with me and my family when he sees us all together."

"He saw our family at the wedding."

"True. But they were well behaved that day. You know how they can all get sometimes. Lydia always wants to be the center of attention, Kitty follows, and then Mother reprimands them." She shook her head. "And then with the Gardiner children running through the house, I have no idea what Will will think." Elizabeth grabbed a cloth to wipe down the counter. "I have the feeling Will is the type of man who prefers peace and quiet over noisy commotion."

Jane dried her hands and then patted her sister's shoulder. "He will be perfectly fine with it."

Elizabeth laughed. "I'll believe that when I see it."

Jane tilted her head. "You really like him, don't you?"

Elizabeth suddenly felt her insides flutter, and she smiled. "I do, Jane. I really do. I was foolish in the beginning to think he was anything like the Gouldings. It was wrong of me to put every wealthy person in that same category." She let out a sigh. "I was not happy to hear about all the hours he worked, but as for his character, I don't think there is anyone finer." She looked at Jane and gave her a reassuring smile. "Except your Charles, of course. The two of them are very fine gentlemen."

Jane nodded with a wide grin. "Yes! I think they both are!"

~~*

Ed and Maddy Gardiner and their family arrived at noon, and the families opened the few gifts they exchanged. They had stopped giving expensive gifts to one another years ago. The younger Gardiner children all received toys, but everyone else was given homemade goods or a gift card to a favorite restaurant or store.

Elizabeth found it difficult to suppress the anticipation she felt about Will's arrival. She glanced about her family home and wondered what he would think of it. She listened to her mother and aunt talking to each other as they worked together in the kitchen. Her Aunt Maddy knew how to keep her mother calm when her nerves seemed on edge. She always admired her for that very reason. She was calm and collected while her mother tended to be nervous and out of control.

When the doorbell rang at precisely one o'clock, Elizabeth's heart lurched. She looked up and saw that everyone's eyes were upon her.

"Well, get up and answer it, Lizzy!" Her mother peeked out from the kitchen. "Don't make him wait."

Elizabeth bit her tongue and sent a forced smile towards her mother but directed a pleading look to Jane as she stood up. She brushed her hands down her sweater and glanced at her reflection in a wall mirror as she walked past. Her heart pounded as she drew close to the door, and when she reached out for the handle, she closed her eyes and drew in a deep breath to calm herself.

"This is ridiculous!" she said softly. She lifted her head, relaxed her shoulders, and smiled.

When she opened the door, she greeted Will and Georgiana warmly. "Merry Christmas! Please come in."

"Thank you," they both replied, stepping in.

Will carried a beautiful red poinsettia, and Georgiana held a decorated box.

"Merry Christmas, Elizabeth." Will said with a smile.

"Thank you," Elizabeth said as she led Will and his sister into the living room, where the adults were sitting. The voices of children could be heard in a room somewhere in the back.

"Will and Georgiana, I know you already met my parents, Tom and Frances, at Jane and Charles's wedding, and this is my aunt and uncle, Ed and Maddy Gardiner."

Frances clasped her hands. "We're delighted you are joining us today."

"It is our pleasure," Georgiana replied.

"Thank you, Mrs. Bennet." Will smiled. "It is good to see you again." He handed her the poinsettia. "This is for your family."

She waved her hand through the air. "Oh, heavens, that is so kind of you!" She took the plant and added, "But please, there is no need for formalities. You must call us Frances and Tom." She beckoned to them. "Please come in and sit down."

They stepped in, and Georgiana held out the box she carried. "We also brought these for all of you. It was very kind of you to invite us for Christmas."

"Thank you," Elizabeth said as she took the box and lifted the lid. Her eyes widened.

"What is it?" Frances asked.

Georgiana smiled. "There are a variety of fine pewter Christmas ornaments with the year inscribed. There are enough for everyone, even fun ones for the children. Each of you can select your own."

Everyone was called into the room to make their selection. Elizabeth saw one that she liked and quickly snatched it up.

"This was so thoughtful of you!" Maddy said, admiring the ornament she selected.

There were more than enough for everyone, and even the children seemed pleased with their gift.

Elizabeth walked to the Christmas tree and pulled out two gift bags, bringing them over. "And these are for you." She handed Georgiana her gift, and Will his.

Georgiana pulled out a basket laden with scented soaps, lotion, and bath bombs. She lifted a bar of soap and sniffed it. "This scent is wonderful! Thank you very much!" She looked at her brother. "What did you get?"

He opened his bag and looked down, laughing. "Ahh! More of the culprit!"

Georgiana looked confused. "Culprit? What is it?"

He pulled out a basket laden with Ardently products. "Let's see, there is an ample supply of after shave, cologne, and soaps."

"I love it on him!" Georgiana exclaimed.

Elizabeth leaned close to her. "I do, too!"

"Thank you, very much. I have worn this for almost two years, and I was wearing it when I was dressed as Santa for PREP's Christmas party. That was how Elizabeth knew it was me."

After the exchange of gifts, the children ran off to play, and

Mary, Kitty, and Lydia disappeared, as well.

The adults visited with each other in the living room, and after a short while, shrill voices and a piece of Christmas music being played on the piano in the next room could be heard. Elizabeth cast a wary glance at Will, wondering what he thought of the commotion. He was engaged in a conversation with Charles and her father, so she hoped he was oblivious to her three younger sisters.

Mary was always inclined to serenade guests with music, especially on Christmas. Elizabeth felt it was her way of avoiding crowds, small talk, and her two younger sisters that made up the triplets. She was eight minutes older, so she always considered herself the oldest and wisest of the three.

Everyone glanced up as Kitty and Lydia scrambled into the room arguing over a knit scarf one of them had received for Christmas.

"I think the green and white looks better on me!" Lydia exclaimed.

"But it's mine! You got the red and white striped one!"

"Girls! Please behave!" Frances shook her finger at them and then pointed to Will and Georgiana.

"Oh!" they both said at once. "Sorry."

Kitty snatched the scarf out of Lydia's hands during the distraction.

Lydia then faced Georgiana. "Are you in college yet?"

"No, I still have another year, but I have begun looking, trying to figure out where I want to go. I understand you both are in college."

"Yes! Let's go to our room, and we'll tell you all about it."

Georgiana sent a questioning look at Will, who nodded his head. She then looked at the others. "Excuse me."

Elizabeth's mother and aunt also excused themselves to return to the kitchen to finish with the dinner preparations.

Elizabeth sat back and enjoyed watching Will engage in conversation with her father and uncle. Her father could carry on a conversation quite well when he wanted, and she was certain her uncle would do the same. Will glanced over at her occasionally giving her a smile, which she returned.

She admired him from the other side of the room, dressed in

jeans and a forest green sweater worn over a light green plaid shirt. He wore the color quite well.

A little later, her mother came out of the kitchen and asked Jane and Elizabeth to help with final meal preparations.

"It must be gravy making time," Jane said as she looked at Elizabeth. "That is Elizabeth's job."

"And your job, my dear sister, is to mash those potatoes to perfection!" She turned to the men. "Would you please excuse us?"

Elizabeth's mother and aunt were busy getting all the items out of the oven or refrigerator and placing them on the long counter. Since they had all worked together to bring about a Christmas dinner for several years, they each knew their task.

When the potatoes were mashed and the gravy was finished, Elizabeth's mother asked her to call her father in. His one duty was to carve the turkey.

Elizabeth stepped back out into the living room, but only her uncle and Charles were there.

"Where is Father?" she asked.

Her uncle pointed to the hallway. "Tom wanted to show Will his library."

Elizabeth smiled, and her brows rose in comprehension. "I see. Thank you." As she walked down the hall, she chuckled. Her father was so proud of his library, but he knew nothing about the library in Will's home - or at least the home in which he grew up.

She stepped into the library to see her father standing behind Will as he perused the bookshelves.

"Very nice," Will said as he drew out a book. "This is a beautiful set of classics."

"Thank you."

"Dad?" Elizabeth said. "Mom needs you in the kitchen."

He laughed. "I knew I would be called in soon." He patted Will on the back. "It is time to carve the turkey. Stay in here as long as you like, although…" He paused and winked at Elizabeth. "If you stay too long, you will likely miss an excellent dinner."

He stepped out, and Elizabeth walked to Will's side. "He loves his library and is very proud of it."

Will returned the book to its place on the shelf. "It is nice." He turned around and faced her, and then looked about the room. "But

I fear… something is missing.”

Elizabeth pinched her brows, and she tilted her head. “Something is missing? You mean there are no first editions? No foreign books written in the original language? Or not enough classics?”

A small smile appeared, and he lifted a brow. “No, nothing like that.” He glanced about the library again and then settled his eyes back on Elizabeth. “There is no mistletoe.”

Elizabeth’s eyes shot open. “No mistletoe? William Darcy, you really seem to have a fascination with mistletoe!”

Will shook his head. “You are wrong.”

“How am I wrong?”

“I have no fascination with it.”

“But you said it was missing from my father’s library.”

“Only because I wanted to kiss you.”

“Do you need the mistletoe to kiss me?” She took a step closer to Will.

“I don’t, but I am not certain whether *you* do.” Will bridged the distance between them and put his arms about her. “For I am of the opinion that we have gone out together at least six times, and a kiss is certainly acceptable.” He lifted a challenging brow.

“I beg to differ, my good sir; we have not been out on even one official date.”

“Semantics, my dear Elizabeth. I consider our first meeting at Derby Steakhouse as the first date, the Christmas Gala as the second, for we did dance a very special waltz together. The third being when we ate lunch together after I installed your computers at PREP, and of course, our evening at the theater, which I will remind you, I did ask you out for that.”

“But you clearly stated it wasn’t a date.”

Will gave a slight shrug and smiled. “I changed my mind.” He glanced upwards and narrowed his eyes as if in thought. “Then there was the wedding, where we waltzed again, and finally, our dining at the Wooden Spoon in Meryton, which, I believe, would be considered a date because you asked me out, and I understand that women do ask men out on dates these days.”

Elizabeth sent him a challenging look. “Are you not counting the time you came to my apartment to return my wallet?”

Will frowned and shook his head. “Heavens, no! I was in no

mood that day to even consider it a date."

"Well, you have certainly presented your case to kiss me." She smiled invitingly.

He drew back. "Are you implying I will have to present my case to you each time I want to kiss you?"

Elizabeth fingered the collar of his shirt. "I might just enjoy hearing your arguments in favor of a kiss."

She tilted her head, and suddenly found herself being pulled close to him. He pressed his lips to hers, running his fingers through her thick, auburn hair. Elizabeth closed her eyes and wrapped her arms about his waist, feeling as though her knees might buckle at any moment.

He reluctantly pulled away after a few moments and drew in a long breath.

Elizabeth leaned her head against his chest and opened her eyes. She looked up at him and smiled. "I think we have just proven that neither of us needs mistletoe."

"And for that, I'm grateful." He leaned over and kissed her again, this time, more briefly. When he pulled back, he looked down at the camphor necklace she was wearing. He brought his fingers up and gently took hold of it. "The necklace looks nice on you, Elizabeth."

She felt a shiver as his hand brushed her neck. She struggled to maintain composure and could barely summon a thought.

"I am glad you like it."

"It makes me think of your grandmother. I really liked her and wish I could have gotten to know her better."

"She was very fond of you, as well."

Elizabeth smiled, but then her expression sobered. "Will, I fear there's something I must warn you about."

"Oh, dear. Are you about to divulge some horrible family secret?"

Elizabeth chuckled. "No, but it does concern my mother. She gets these notions in her head whenever any one of her daughters begins dating someone. She becomes relentless about how perfect a couple they make, or how she is certain there will soon be an engagement or marriage." She brought her hands up to his chest. "Therefore, I caution you against displaying any signs of affection that she might interpret as there being something between us."

Will's eyes held hers. "Are you of the opinion there is nothing between us?"

Elizabeth's mouth dried, and she could barely think. "I… I just don't… Will, things are only just beginning with us. We need time, and that is something my mother won't give us if she suspects anything."

"Heard and understood." He smiled and kissed her once more. He drew away and clasped her hand in his. "There, that ought to last me until next time." He looked towards the door. "I suppose we ought to go see if dinner is ready."

Elizabeth put up her hand. "Not quite yet. I have a Christmas gift for you and thought I would give it to you in here."

"You don't want your mother to see that you are giving me a gift?"

"Well, partly." She pulled out a small, wrapped gift from her sweater pocket and handed it to him.

"You already gave me a good supply of Ardently."

"That was technically from my family."

He began to pull off the paper, occasionally looking at her as he did. When he opened the small box, he smiled. "A tiny bottle of… hot sauce?"

She laughed. "It is actually part of a set of 24 different sauces with different levels of… hotness." She laughed. "You said you like things hot. Just don't expect me to sample all of them with you."

"Well, I thank you." He lifted a brow. "And I do like things hot." His eyes twinkled.

She felt her cheeks warm. "I will give you the whole set later."

"By the way, Elizabeth, I didn't see what ornament you selected."

"Oh, I pocketed it right away. I was so excited when I saw it." She reached into her pocket, pulled out the ornament, and held it out to Will.

"Ahh, the dancing couple. I was hoping you would see this one. Do you think they're dancing the waltz?"

"Of course, they are, and the music playing is *The Christmas Waltz*."

Will placed two fingers under her chin and lifted her face to his. "I hope we can repeat that waltz together someday."

Her breath caught. "I do, too."

Will leaned down and placed a brief kiss on her lips.

When he lifted his head, they gazed at each other for a moment in silence.

Elizabeth finally said, "Shall we see if dinner is ready?"

Will extended his arm towards the door. "After you."

Chapter 20

The dinner was excellent, and everyone seemed to enjoy it. The turkey was succulent, the potatoes were mashed to perfection, the gravy was creamy, and the biscuits were light and airy. The table was a little crowded, with eleven adults, so Mary offered to sit at the table with the Gardiners' children.

After the meal, Frances invited everyone back into the living room while she and Maddy began cleaning up and getting the desserts ready. The aroma of freshly baked apple, pecan, and pumpkin pies wafted through the house.

Jane and Charles sat together on a small loveseat that they had occupied all morning. Elizabeth sat down on one of the extra folding chairs that had been brought out earlier, and Will sat next to her in a plush armchair. He sat forward in the chair, as if to draw closer to her. She was grateful he was just far enough away in the hopes her mother wouldn't begin speculating about them.

Mary began playing Christmas music again, but this time there seemed to be something different. Elizabeth peered into the den and noticed that Georgiana had joined her at the piano.

She looked back at everyone. "Georgiana and Mary are playing a duet!"

Tom Bennet laughed. "Well, that explains that! Mary's playing has never sounded better!"

They sat in silence as the two performed a lovely rendition of "O Holy Night," and then continued to play a medley of Christmas carols.

Later, Frances and Maddy came out with trays laden with plates, pies, vanilla ice cream, and whipped cream. They placed them on a table, where everyone helped themselves. Elizabeth noticed Will whispering to Charles, who then looked over at her and smiled. She wondered what the two men were up to.

They all returned to sit down with their desserts, but instead of going over to the loveseat, Charles ushered Jane to the large sofa. Will walked to the loveseat and extended his hand inviting Elizabeth to join him there.

She quickly glanced at her mother, who fortunately didn't see his gesture. She walked over and sat down, hoping not to attract her mother's attention. But she knew that would likely be impossible. And she was correct.

When Frances turned around, her eyes widened at seeing Will and her daughter sitting so close. A wide smile appeared, and she winked at Elizabeth. Elizabeth hoped Will had not seen.

They finished eating their desserts, and Frances walked around to collect the empty plates.

"Were the pies to your satisfaction?" Frances directed her question to Will.

"Everything has been wonderful. The pies, the turkey… the gravy!" He turned to Elizabeth with a smile.

"Oh, Lizzy made the gravy! That is her specialty! But she also baked the apple pie." A wide smile lit her face. "There is no finer cook than our Lizzy."

"Mother, I don't think…" Elizabeth stopped when she felt Will's arm go behind her. She stiffened when she felt his hand rest on her shoulder, not because his touch was repulsive. It was anything but. It did, however, cause a look of delight to cross her mother's face.

"That is great to hear!" He turned his head and looked at Elizabeth, a twinkle in his eyes. "I believe I will have to keep my eye on this one." He smiled, and she felt Will give her shoulder a few light pats. He then reached over with his other hand and took hers in his.

She turned back to her mother who looked like she was about to speak again. Her aunt whispered something to her and ushered her out of the room. *Thank goodness for Aunt Maddy*!

She sent Will a stern look. "You don't know how lucky we both are that my aunt is here!" Elizabeth spoke in a whisper. "I warned you…"

He lifted a brow. "I was actually hoping to hear what she might say."

Elizabeth shook her head. "Will, you surprise me. I had no idea you had such a mischievous streak in you."

At that moment, Georgiana stepped back into the room. "Will, it is about time for us to leave. You told me to remind you."

Will looked at his watch. "Yes, it is. Thank you, Georgie." He turned to Elizabeth. "I promised her I'd let her go to her friend's home for the evening."

Elizabeth felt a sudden pang of disappointment and forced a smile. "Oh, certainly! I'm pleased you both came."

He stood. "Come, Georgiana. Let's thank the Bennets and let them know we're leaving." He turned back to Elizabeth. "Would you be so kind as to accompany us outside?"

Elizabeth nodded and then waited for Will and Georgiana to express their thanks and goodbyes.

The three walked out quietly, and at the car, Will opened the door for Georgiana, who slipped in. He took Elizabeth's hand and walked with her towards the back of the car.

He smiled and pressed his lips together. He drew in a breath and then asked, "Would it be okay if I came by your place after dropping Georgiana off?" His eyes pleaded with her.

"I would very much like that. I can give you the rest of your Christmas gift then."

Her response was met with a wide grin. "Good!" Glancing down at his watch, he asked, "Will you be home by seven?"

"I should be. I will be waiting for you."

Elizabeth stood and watched as the car drove away. She couldn't help but feel anticipation that she'd be seeing him again in just a few hours. When she turned back towards the house, her mind took a different turn. As soon as she walked in, her mother would be pressing her about their relationship and insisting upon knowing everything about this fine young man whom she believed was decidedly in love with her daughter.

Elizabeth smiled. For once in her life, she didn't care.

~~*

Later that evening, Elizabeth waited in her apartment for Will to arrive. She was looking forward to some time alone with him – away from her family. After he had left, her mother had been relentless in her questions, assumptions, and conjectures about the possibility of a marriage between them. It was, in her own words,

"The most wonderful thing she could ever imagine."

When the doorbell rang, Elizabeth took in a deep breath and walked to the door, stopping briefly to glance into the mirror. She ran her fingers across the top of her head, straightening some wayward strands of hair, and licked her recently glossed lips.

She opened the door and welcomed Will with a beaming smile. "Come in," she said, glancing down at the briefcase he was holding. He was also holding a small box, which he handed to her. "This is for you. Merry Christmas."

She looked at him. "You didn't have to. She fingered her camphor necklace. You already gave me this."

Will shook his head. "No, my grandmother gave that to you."

She opened the box and lifted out a plaque. As she read it, tears came to her eyes. She looked up at him. "PREP Music Room - In memory of Melissa." She looked up. "Oh, Will! This is amazing!"

"I thought you could put it just inside your new music room or possibly right outside the door. You did say Melissa was very fond of music, didn't you?"

"Oh, yes! And she was very gifted. I know she would have…" Elizabeth's voice trailed off as she choked back the words.

Will wrapped his arms about her. "I hoped you would like it."

Elizabeth returned his hug. "I do, Will. I couldn't have asked for anything better."

She reached behind her and gave Will a gift bag that held the remaining twenty-three small bottles of hot sauce. "Here are your remaining presents!"

"Thank you. I shall enjoy trying them all out!" He turned to his briefcase and opened it. "Now, I want you to look at this." He pulled out a roll of papers. "This is the floor plan of the two stories in the building that is being considered to purchase for PREP once you approve. I want you to have fun designing where you want the rooms and how you want it set up. Walls can always be added, and unless a wall is a load-bearing wall, it can likely be removed."

She looked up in awe. "Can I really do that?"

"I want you to do that. The architects will have to do the final draft and see if what you want is something they can do, but this will be a great start!"

Elizabeth placed her hand over her heart and let out a long sigh. "I really can't believe this. I don't even know where to begin."

He laughed. "I brought extras if you want to experiment with different floorplans. Just go for it!"

"Oh, I most certainly will!"

He then pulled out some other papers.

"What are these?"

"These are the drawings and aerial photographs of a four-square block set of homes in the Longbourn Downs area, just a few streets away from PREP's new location. It is something that was begun a few years ago but stalled due to a lack of finances." He looked up. "Have you heard of the Longbourn Restoration Initiative?"

She shook her head.

"The homes in this area are all old Victorian style houses, and many of the residents are beginning to restore their neighborhood to the glory of earlier years. It is what I would like F&D Foundation to pursue for our next endeavor. The houses would remain with the owners as they work to improve them and their neighborhood. Funding will come from different corporations who want to invest in this part of town. I know of several that are specifically looking to invest in lower income housing areas."

He then pulled out some pictures from his briefcase. "These are some of the individual houses. Many have great potential."

Elizabeth chuckled. "What I would give to live in one of these."

"Well," Will drawled as he flipped through the pictures. "A few of these are vacant. These two, and…" He pointed to a third one. "This one has an empty lot next to it that could become part of the property." Elizabeth took the picture of that house as he flipped through more photos. "And this is a picture of two lots with houses that are abandoned and beyond repair. Richard and I thought they could be bulldozed, and a park could be made for the area."

"Oh, Will! This is amazing!" She clutched the picture of the one vacant house. "This is my favorite. It has so much potential." She laughed. "What do I have to do to get this one for me?"

Will put the pictures down and rested his arms on her shoulders, drawing her close. He leaned over and kissed the tip of her nose. "While I would advise you to actually walk through the house before you make a decision, I am certain, my dear Elizabeth, that it can be negotiated."

Will looked at her and drew in a deep breath. "Elizabeth, we teased each other earlier about whether or not we'd ever been on a real date, but I can't hold in my feelings any longer. I... I love you. I love you very much and have loved you for some time!"

Elizabeth's heart raced as she heard his heartfelt words.

Will unexpectedly chuckled.

"What do you find so humorous?" Elizabeth asked.

"I told you I fell in love with you when you blurted out, 'It's not *Snobs* on the Hill!' the first night we met."

She looked at him and a wide smile lit her face. "I can't believe you first fell in love with me when you heard me say that."

"Well, I did, and my love for you has only deepened every time we have been together."

Elizabeth shuddered, barely able to conjure up a single thought. Mindful of the lump of emotion swelling inside of her, however, there was something she needed to say. "Will, while it may have been longer in coming, I am hopelessly in love with you."

Will smiled and let out a breath he seemed to have been holding. "And when did you fall in love with me?"

"Oh, dear! It's hard to say! For I kept trying to talk myself out of it." She looked up to meet his gaze. "I had stirrings of disappointment when you told me you had not intended to ask me to dance at Derby's. Then I had stirrings of disappointment when you told me you'd asked me to waltz at the Gala only because I was the first one you encountered after Georgiana told you she was going to dance with her boyfriend."

Elizabeth continued. "I knew I was falling in love with you when you pulled away in the classic convertible at Charles and Jane's wedding, and I despaired that I'd never see you again. It made it even more difficult every time Charles and Jane spoke about you – and spoke so highly about you!" She gently pressed her palms against his chest, feeling his beating heart. "Dare I say I am so grateful Richard got sick the day of PREP's Christmas party, and you had to fill in as Santa?" She let out a long sigh. "And yes, I did ask you out to the Wooden Spoon after the party because I didn't want to risk losing you again."

Will took her hands in his and brought them to his lips, kissing each one. He looked into her eyes and whispered, "I love you more than anything, Elizabeth Bennet." He then wrapped his arms about her and pulled her close, kissing her soundly and passionately.

Chapter 21

The Following December

Jane stood behind Elizabeth, admiring her sister's reflection in the mirror. "You look beautiful!"

"Yes, she certainly does!" their mother exclaimed excitedly. "And that fine man you are marrying will certainly make you very happy! He will provide well for you!"

"Thank you, Mother," Elizabeth said with a sigh of resignation. She knew her mother was speaking mainly of his money.

There was a tap at the door, and Charlotte announced herself.

"Come in, Charlotte!" Elizabeth said.

Charlotte entered with her clipboard. She looked at Frances. "It is about time for the family to be seated, so you need to proceed to the back doors of the sanctuary."

Frances clasped her hands. "Oh, my goodness! It is almost time." She leaned over and gave Elizabeth a kiss on her cheek. "You have made me so happy!"

Elizabeth watched her mother leave, and she gave a slight shrug. "I hope that once we are married, she will end her litany of praise for his wealth. I would prefer she praise his character, his generosity, his kindness…" Her voice trailed. "How wrong I was about him in the beginning… because of that wealth." She chuckled softly. "Mother and I have such different views."

"He does seem to be a good man," Charlotte said. "So, are you ready to become Mrs. Darcy?"

"I believe I am. It took me long enough to realize how good he is."

Jane patted her sister's shoulder. "And just think of everything that has happened in this past year. You moved PREP into its new facility, added to your staff, got engaged, have a newly remodeled home, and are now getting married."

Elizabeth laughed. "I feel so very blessed, and although our home isn't quite finished, it will soon be livable."

Charlotte leaned in. "Now, I've gone through my checklist, but have you gone through yours?"

"Mine?"

"Yes. You know - something old, something new, something borrowed, and something blue."

Elizabeth obediently pointed to her diamond earrings. "Borrowed from Mother." She patted her leg. "And my garter is laced with a blue ribbon and small blue flowers." Her fingers touched the camphor necklace around her neck. "This is definitely old, and something I will always treasure."

"And it looks beautiful with your organza dress. What about the new?"

Elizabeth smiled and lifted her arm to reveal a white gold diamond bracelet. "From Will." She began to play with the bracelet, twirling it around her wrist. "Normally I'd consider it a little too extravagant for me, but he had it inscribed inside with something very special, and I absolutely love it!"

"What does it say?" Charlotte asked.

She smiled. "Elizabeth, may we forever waltz through this life together. Love, Will."

"That is sweet. I hope to see the two of you waltz at your reception." She turned to walk out. "Well, I better make sure the family gets seated - and in the right place! I'll come back to get you in a few minutes."

Once she left, Elizabeth took Jane's hands. "I have you to thank for helping me see Will in a different light. You and Charles were always speaking highly of him in one way or another."

Jane's brows lifted conspiratorially. "Well, my dearest sister, that was our intent. We knew Will's feelings for you were very strong, but that would not have made a bit of difference if you felt he cared more about his money and his job than anything else."

"He is very generous with his money."

Jane laughed, and Elizabeth asked her what she found humorous.

"Oh, it is just that Will's penchant for giving his money away is what drove Caroline away. She couldn't understand why he would step down from such a lucrative position only to work for a foundation to give money away."

"Better for her to have found that out before anything happened between them."

"Nothing would have ever happened between them!" Jane exclaimed. "Will was very forthright about his feelings for her. Or perhaps I should say his lack of feelings for her." She gave a shrug. "I think Caroline still harbors some resentment. She made some silly excuse for not coming to the wedding today."

"I can understand it. All her hopes and dreams were tied up in the wealthy Will Darcy and everything she could have if she married him."

"She could not believe the two of you bought a home in Longbourn Downs. She blames you for having an undue influence on him."

"It is unfortunate she does not know the true man." Elizabeth clasped her hands and looked at Jane. "I love the way our house has come along. And the neighbors are so friendly and excited about what a great area it will be to raise a family."

"I'm glad you bought the empty lot next to your house to give yourself a large yard. What fun it will be for your children and ours to play there together." Jane smiled and placed her hands on her belly. "I hope the two of you will soon follow in our footsteps and give our baby a cousin."

"Give us a little time to get used to married life, first," Elizabeth said with a chuckle. "Have you told anyone else yet?"

Jane shook her head. "No. We've only told you and Will. We'll probably announce our exciting news to everyone else in a week or two."

Charlotte returned, announcing, "It's time. Shall we go?"

~~*

Elizabeth and Jane walked with Charlotte to the back of the church where they joined their father, who smiled upon seeing them.

"My! I don't think I have seen the two of you look so beautiful since…" He paused and smiled. "Well, since Jane's wedding!"

"Thank you, Father," they both said at once.

He took Elizabeth's hands in his. "My dear Lizzy, I couldn't be more delighted with that young man you are marrying. Oh, he is rich, to be sure, as your mother knows quite well and often reminds me, but he is so much more than that. He has a humble, generous, and caring side of him that is often lacking in young men today."

"Yes, he does," Elizabeth said. "I'm so grateful you see that!" She leaned in and kissed his cheek.

Charlotte peeked through the doors at the back of the church and looked in. "Everything is ready. Are you?"

The three nodded.

"Good! I will signal for the musicians to begin playing, and Jane, you can step out."

Mary and Georgiana began playing a duet on the piano, soon to be joined by Richard on the flute.

Charlotte closed the doors behind Jane and watched for her to reach the front.

Charlotte turned back. "It is time. Once you walk down that aisle, Elizabeth, there is no turning back."

Elizabeth smiled. "I would have it no other way!"

The three musicians began to play the processional, and Charlotte opened the doors wide to reveal Elizabeth and her father. The guests stood and turned towards them as they began their walk.

The church had already been decorated for the advent season with lighted trees, poinsettias, and bright red ribbons and bows. For the wedding, an arch had been set up in front, decorated with greenery, hanging ribbons, berries, and pinecones. The lights had dimmed, and the candles lining her path flickered as she walked past them.

But Elizabeth didn't notice any of these things. A small spotlight illuminated the front of the church, and her eyes settled on Will. She couldn't take them off him.

She felt such a thrill of excitement and anticipation, that she almost wished she could run up to him. But no, she remembered Charlotte's admonition to walk slowly, to allow everyone an opportunity to see her.

She had to force herself to turn to them and smile, reminding herself that in less than an hour, she and Will would be married, and he would always be by her side.

As she drew closer, she sensed that Will felt the same

eagerness. He was leaning forward, as if willing to bridge the distance between them. His eyes were locked with hers with an intensity she once believed was arrogance but had later discovered stemmed from a deep admiration for her.

At the front, her father handed her off to Will. When he took her hand in his, he gave it a squeeze. Her hand, encased in his, felt warm and secure. The minister was speaking, welcoming everyone, but she heard little of what he said.

They recited their vows, exchanged rings, and Mary, Georgiana, and Richard played one more song. As the minister pronounced them husband and wife and announced that Will could kiss his bride, Will paused and looked at her, admiration in his eyes. As he lowered his head, he whispered, "I love you," and placed a warm, lingering, and soft kiss on her lips.

When he drew away, Elizabeth smiled up at him and whispered, "I love you, too."

They turned to face their guests as the music began to play for their exit.

Once outside the doors, and before Jane and Charles joined them, Will drew Elizabeth into his arms and kissed her soundly. When he drew back, he pressed his forehead to hers. "My dearest, loveliest, Elizabeth! You have made me so very happy!"

Elizabeth smiled. "And I couldn't be happier!"

The guests were invited to proceed to the reception, which was about a twenty-minute drive from the church. Meanwhile, the bride and groom and their families stayed back for photographs. It was decided that the meal would be served shortly after the guests arrived so they wouldn't have to wait.

When Will and Elizabeth finally arrived at the reception venue, they were announced by Richard, who was acting as the emcee. Everyone stood and applauded as they entered.

The reception was being held in a banquet hall on the 7th floor of the office building which housed Darcy Enterprises. A beautiful and popular venue for receptions and other large events, it was decorated with tiny white twinkling lights around the room and that covered a large Christmas tree, which was also filled with red and gold ornaments.

White tablecloths covered the rectangular tables where the guests were seated, and the center of each table held a small wreath of live evergreen, a large glass candle holder containing a red candle, baby's breath, and two poinsettias on either side. Lively instrumental Christmas music played in the background.

The tables set up for the wedding party were situated directly in front of the tree, and Will and Elizabeth greeted some of the guests as they walked to their seats. They were seated with Charles and Jane as well as some of their families. Richard was seated between Mary and Kitty, and across from Lydia. By their laughter, it seemed all three girls were highly entertained by him. Georgiana was on the other side of Mary, and the friendship they had formed over the past year and more recently in practicing for the wedding, had continued to grow.

At length, Richard got up to perform his duty as the emcee for the evening. He began with a toast, then turned the microphone over to Charles and Jane, who each shared something special about the newly married couple. He then directed everyone to the floor, where Elizabeth threw her bouquet, which was caught by Kamie, and Will threw Elizabeth's garter, which was caught by Richard.

Richard prodded Will and Elizabeth in the cutting of their cake, hoping for at least one of them to get a mouthful all over their faces, but it was not to be. They were very proper as they fed one another their piece of cake.

Then Richard asked the couple to join him. He began to tell everyone the story about their first dance and the song this couple had chosen for their first dance as husband and wife.

"Some of you may already know this, but the first time Will and Elizabeth danced together was at his family's Christmas Gala. He had asked Elizabeth to dance the traditional first waltz when his sister Georgiana, who was supposed to dance with him, told him she was going to dance with her boyfriend." Richard sent a pointed look to Georgiana, and the guests all laughed.

"Now I was out of town that night and didn't witness the dance, but they danced to the song, *The Christmas Waltz*. I believe – and I have it on good authority – that during that dance, or maybe by the end of it, Will was hopelessly in love." He looked at his cousin. "Is that correct, Will?"

Will turned and smiled at Elizabeth and then looked back. "How could I not have fallen in love with her?"

"Ah, but there we have the conundrum!" Richard said.

"Elizabeth had no intention of falling in love with Will, and it would be a full year before there was any major change in the lady's feelings towards him." He looked at Elizabeth. "Is that correct?"

"I would have to say that my feelings for him changed quite a few times that following year." Again, everyone laughed.

"So tonight, as their first dance as a married couple, they will waltz to the song, *The Christmas Waltz*, as they did that night. Everyone, enjoy Will and Elizabeth Darcy on the dance floor."

The music began, and they began to waltz. Elizabeth felt much more confident this time, especially since they had danced it again at this year's Gala and had many opportunities to practice it together leading up to the Gala and tonight.

When the song came to an end, he dipped her, and everyone applauded. He leaned down and kissed her, bringing her slowly up.

The reception continued into the evening, with Will and Elizabeth dancing a few more times, but often taking the time to meet and greet their guests.

Later, as they were once again on the dance floor, Will nodded his head to the side. "I do believe there is another couple in the making here."

"What?" asked Elizabeth, as she turned to see Richard and Kamie dancing. "Oh, I am so glad! Kamie really liked Richard when he first came to PREP dressed as Santa!" Elizabeth chuckled. "Even though she couldn't see what he looked like. She told me she hoped he would be Santa at our Christmas party this year. I told her she wouldn't have to wait for the party to see him again, as he would be at our wedding. I did encourage her to make an effort to get to know him today!"

"Well, he confessed to me that he liked her, as well, and I encouraged him to get to know her."

Elizabeth smiled. "It looks as though they are enjoying each other's company." She paused and then said, "Perhaps they are only talking about the logistics for the up-coming Christmas party."

Will gave a shrug. "Perhaps, but I highly doubt it."

Kamie looked her way, and Elizabeth gave her a smiling nod. Elizabeth turned back to Will. "I think they'll make a great couple!"

At the end of the evening, Will and Elizabeth changed out of their wedding clothes, and were sent off by their guests waving twinkling sparklers.

They got into one of the Darcy family's antique cars, but instead of having someone drive them, Will took the wheel. He told Elizabeth that while it would be nice to sit in the backseat with her and with someone else driving, he wished to be alone with her and drive himself.

Their plans were to fly out the next morning to Vermont, where they would stay at an exclusive inn. They'd have access to skiing, sledding, cross-country skiing, an indoor pool and jacuzzi, and a beautiful view from their room. But he had kept secret where they were spending their wedding night.

"Are you ever going to tell me where we're staying?" Elizabeth asked as they drove away. "I would have been perfectly content to stay in our house, even though it isn't completely finished."

Will reached over and took her hand. "I know, but I wanted something special, memorable." He gave it a squeeze. "Only the best for my Elizabeth."

A short while later, when Will's blinker indicated he was turning off the highway, Elizabeth gasped and let out a laugh. "Will! Don't tell me…"

He looked over at her with a smile. "I hope you don't mind."

"Hobbs on the Hill?" She laughed and shook her head. "I should have known!"

"Trust me, I think you'll enjoy it! It does place us closer to the airport, so we won't have too far to drive in the morning. Unfortunately, we won't be able to eat at the restaurant since it is too late tonight, and we'll be leaving too early in the morning, but I hope you'll enjoy the accommodations well enough to give the restaurant a chance sometime in the future. Maybe?" He lifted his brows in question.

Elizabeth laughed. "Maybe."

They reached the top of the hill and Will pulled the car to valet parking. An attendant opened the doors, and Will took the one small bag they had for the evening. Their luggage for their honeymoon was secure in the trunk.

Will had come by earlier in the day to check in, so they went directly to their room, which was located on the fifth floor. When they stepped inside, Elizabeth gasped. It was beautiful. A gas fire was lit in the fireplace, flames dancing about. A round table with a floor length tablecloth was filled with delectable fruits, bread and cheese, candles, greenery, and a small Christmas tree decorated with miniature ornaments and lights.

Will escorted Elizabeth to the double sliding glass doors. He opened them, and they stepped out onto the balcony.

"Oh, Will, the view is amazing!"

The lights from the city below, both from the regular lights and the array of Christmas lights, danced and sparkled in the dark, winter night.

"It is, isn't it?" He glanced up. "Unfortunately, the cloudy sky is hiding all the stars above. Because there isn't as much light up here as there is down in the city, the stars themselves can put on quite a show."

Elizabeth tucked her arm through his. "Then perhaps you will have to bring me back up here on a cloudless night." She leaned against him.

Will leaned down and kissed the top of her head. "Gladly!"

He put his arm about her, and they watched in silence, warmed by the presence of each other. A chilly breeze swept across them, and when Elizabeth felt a snowflake touch her nose, she laughed. "Look! It's beginning to snow."

Will glanced up. "I believe you are right," he replied and put his arms about her. "Perhaps we ought to go inside where it is warmer." His gaze lingered on her.

Elizabeth snuggled up against him. She tilted her head, looking up at him. "While I'm quite warm in your embrace, I agree it would be wise to return inside." She glanced towards the window and nodded her head in that direction. "It appears there is a very large, plump chair situated directly in front of the fireplace." She arched her brows invitingly, a mischievous glint in her eyes. "It looks very inviting."

Will smiled. "That chair is large, but I believe for us to sit in it together, you may just have to sit on my lap."

"Oh, no, my dearest husband. I definitely *will* have to sit on your lap." She brought her arms up and locked her fingers around his neck. "Shall we?"

"Just one more thing," Will said. He lowered his head and kissed her, as he pulled her even closer to him. He drew back and gently wiped a snowflake from her face, kissing the cool spot where it had landed. "I love you. You mean the world to me, Elizabeth, and I can think of nothing that could have made me happier than having you as my wife." He brought his hands up and combed his fingers through her dark, auburn hair. "My greatest wish, and my promise to you this evening, is that I will do everything in my power to ensure your happiness as we waltz through this life together."

Elizabeth looked down at the engraved bracelet she still wore and smiled. She turned to kiss one of his hands that was still within the locks of her hair. "At the moment, I am the happiest I have ever been." She pressed her cheek against his palm. "And it is solely because of you, Will Darcy. I love you more than anything." She let out a long, soft sigh. "More than anything."

~ THE END ~

ABOUT THE AUTHOR

Kara Louise grew up in the San Fernando Valley in Southern California, but now lives in the suburbs of St. Louis, Missouri with her husband, and their ever-changing number of pets. Their son, his wife, and their three daughters live nearby, so her time is often spent being 'Nana' to them.

Other books by Kara Louise:

Pemberley's Promise
Something Like Regret
Assumed Engagement
Assumed Obligation
Drive and Determination
Master Under Good Regulation
Pemberley Celebrations: The First Year
Pirates and Prejudice
Mr. Darcy's Rival
A Peculiar Engagement
Chance and Circumstance
Mr. Darcy's Magpie
and
Encounter to Remember

~~*

www.karalouise.net